"I didn't file for divorce, Savannah. You did."

Bewildered, she stared into his eyes, seeming to be searching for answers. "I did? Why? Why would I do that?"

"We had a lot of problems we just couldn't seem to work out," he told her honestly.

Savannah covered her face with her hands. In a muffled voice, she said, "I just want to go home."

Bruce moved to her side; sitting on the edge of the bed, he pulled her hands down from her face and tugged her gently into his arms so he could comfort her in the only way he knew how. He ran his hand over the back of her hair, the way she always liked him to, and was relieved that instead of drawing away from him, Savannah leaned against him and rested her head on his shoulder.

"Come home to me, Savannah." Bruce hugged his wife, his eyes closed.

Savannah broke the embrace and studied his face, looked directly into his eyes again when she asked him, "Do you still love me?"

The cowboy answered firmly and without any hesitation, "Yes, beautiful. Yes, I do."

* * *

T**** ***** ** MONTANA:
Wrang*** **** ****** **** ****ors

Dear Reader,

Thank you for choosing *A Wedding to Remember*! This is my ninth Special Edition book featuring the Brand family, which is an honor for me. I'm excited to introduce you to a whole new branch of the Brands. *A Wedding to Remember* introduces readers to the Brands of Sugar Creek Ranch, a sprawling working cattle ranch outside Bozeman, Montana. Jock Brand is the patriarch of the Bozeman Brands, and he has fathered eight children from two marriages. I am looking forward to bringing you stories about each and every one of them!

A Wedding to Remember features Bruce Brand and his wife, Savannah. These two star-crossed lovers are on the verge of divorce when Savannah is in a near-fatal car accident. This accident is the catalyst that brings about a return to love for Bruce and Savannah, whose marriage had been torn apart by a tragedy. *A Wedding to Remember* is a second-chance story; a story about redemption, forgiveness and renewing a commitment to marriage. I love writing second-chance stories and I hope that you will love *A Wedding to Remember*!

I invite you to visit my website, joannasimsromance. com, and while you're there, be sure to sign up for *Rendezvous Magazine* for Brand-family extras, news and swag. Part of the joy of writing is hearing from readers. If you write me, I will write you back! That's a promise.

Happy reading!

Joanna

A Wedding to Remember

———

Joanna Sims

 **HARLEQUIN**®SPECIAL EDITION®

Recycling programs
for this product may
not exist in your area.

ISBN-13: 978-0-373-62372-3

A Wedding to Remember

Copyright © 2017 by Joanna Sims

Printed in U.S.A.

www.Harlequin.com

Joanna Sims is proud to pen contemporary romance for Harlequin Special Edition. Joanna's series, The Brands of Montana, features hardworking characters with hometown values. You are cordially invited to join the Brands of Montana as they wrangle their own happily-ever-afters. And, as always, Joanna welcomes you to visit her at her website: joannasimsromance.com.

Books by Joanna Sims

Harlequin Special Edition

The Brands of Montana

Thankful For You
Meet Me at the Chapel
High Country Baby
High Country Christmas
A Match Made in Montana

Marry Me, Mackenzie!
The One He's Been Looking For
A Baby for Christmas

Visit the Author Profile page
at Harlequin.com for more titles.

Dedicated to my dear friend Madhu.
An exceptional woman
who recently rediscovered romance.
I love you.

Chapter One

"Hello?"

It was the middle of the night, but for the last week Bruce Brand had been sleeping lightly, waiting for any news from the hospital. Savannah, his soon-to-be-ex-wife, had been in a coma after a near-fatal car accident.

"She's awake." It was Carol, his mother-in-law, on the other end of the call.

Bruce tossed the covers off his body, sat up on the edge of the bed and dropped his head into the palm of his free hand. "Thank God. *Jesus*—thank God."

"She's been asking for you," Carol added after a pause.

Bruce lifted his head in surprise. "Asking for *me*?"

"Yes," Carol confirmed matter-of-factly. "Will you come?"

"I'm on my way."

Not thinking, just acting, Bruce stood up as he was ending the call. He grabbed his jeans, which were draped over a chair in the corner of the room, and tugged them on. With his jeans pulled up but still unzipped, he pushed the pillows off the chair, sat down and shoved his foot into his boot.

"What's going on?" Kerri, the woman he'd been dating for the last six months or so, flipped on the light.

"Savannah's awake." Bruce rose after his boots were on.

In the yellow glow of the lamp, the nipples of her full, naked breasts peeking through her wavy, sun-bleached blond hair, Kerri wore an expression of disappointment mixed with resignation on her pretty girl-next-door face.

"And she asked for you," Kerri stated in a monotone as she pulled the sheet up over her breasts and held it in place with her arms pinned to her sides.

Bruce didn't bother tucking in his T-shirt; he ran his fingers through the front of his silver-laced black hair several times to push it off his forehead before he put his cowboy hat on. He checked to make sure his wallet was in his back pocket, then grabbed the keys to his truck off the top of the dresser.

"I'm sorry. I have to go." When he leaned in to kiss her on the lips, she turned her head so her mouth was just out of reach.

Bruce straightened; he understood Kerri well enough to know that this was the beginning of a fight they were going to have later.

Kerri looked up at him, and he genuinely regretted the raw hurt he could easily read in her eyes.

"If this hadn't happened," Kerri reminded him, "you'd already be divorced."

She was right about that. He'd spent the last two years paying for his lawyer to fight with Savannah's lawyer. He'd received the final draft of the divorce agreement a couple of days before the accident. For now, the divorce was on hold. And, even though they hadn't lived as man and wife for years, legally he was Savannah's husband.

"She's still my wife," Bruce paused in the doorway to say. "I'll call when I can."

The night of Savannah's accident, and every day since, had felt more like a surreal dream sequence than reality. For the last week, when he wasn't working, he was with the Scott family, crammed into the small waiting room designated for families who had a loved one in the critical care unit. Truth be told, he'd never expected to speak to any of Savannah's kin again, much less spend several hours a day in a confined space with them drinking burnt coffee out of a Styrofoam cup and trying to make sense out of the sudden detour his life had just taken.

When he arrived at the hospital, the feeling in the waiting room had changed dramatically from somber to celebratory. Savannah's two sisters, Joy and Justine, were smiling with tears of relief and happiness drying on their faces. The peaches-and-cream color had returned to Carol's plump face, and John, Savannah's burly father, was actually smiling broadly enough so that the tips of his upper teeth, normally hidden from view behind his thick salt-and-pepper mustache and beard, were visible. But there was one person in the room who didn't seem to be happy at all.

"Hi, Carol." Bruce stopped next to Carol and the cowboy Savannah had been dating. He didn't offer his hand when he said, "Leroy."

Beside the fact that the cowpoke was dating his wife, Bruce had a hard time keeping his cool around Leroy. It was Leroy's high-powered muscle car that Savannah had been driving the night of the accident. Leroy had been in the passenger seat and had walked away from the accident with a broken wrist and a couple of scrapes and bruises, while Savannah had shattered the windshield with her skull.

Leroy had a stricken look on his narrow face. "She doesn't remember me."

Carol put her hand on Leroy's arm to comfort him. "She will, Leroy. The doctor said that it may take a couple of days. We just have to be patient and give her some time."

The cowpoke left with his head bent down, and it occurred to Bruce, for the first time, that Leroy was in love with Savannah.

"What's he talking about?" he asked Carol.

The Scott clan closed ranks and surrounded him as if they were worried he would try to escape.

Now Carol's hand was on his arm. "Savannah's neurologist thinks she may be experiencing some…temporary memory loss."

No one spoke for a second, but all of the Scotts were watching him like a cat watching fish in a fishbowl. "How temporary?"

"They don't know." John spoke directly to him for

the first time, instead of communicating through his wife and daughters as was his usual route.

"Bruce." Carol's fingers tightened on his arm. "Savannah doesn't seem to remember the divorce."

Until right then, Bruce hadn't felt like he needed to sit down. Now he did. Wordlessly, he took a couple of steps backward and settled in a nearby chair.

Savannah's family moved as one unit as they followed him, making loud scraping noises on the floor as they pulled chairs closer to him, boxing him in again. Bruce realized now that Savannah's tight-knit family wasn't trying to protect him—they were trying to make sure he didn't leave.

As much as his in-laws knew about Savannah's condition and potential recovery, they shared with him. Savannah was awake and talking; her speech was a little slurred, but she was making sense. But she had lost, at least temporarily, memory of the last several years. As far as Savannah was concerned, there was no divorce, they hadn't spent the last two years fighting through their lawyers and she had never moved out of their home. In her mind, they were still happily married. Now he understood why she had been asking for him. Savannah needed her husband.

Waking up from a coma had felt like swimming up to the surface from the bottom of a seemingly bottomless pool. Savannah had felt tingly all over right before the awareness of the throbbing, stabbing pain coming from the left side of her head along with the achiness and stiffness that she felt all over the rest of her body. She had been petrified, unable to understand why she was in a hospital hooked up to monitors with needles in her arms. She didn't have any memory of the accident; the last thing she could remember was kissing Bruce goodbye as he left to start his day on the Brand family ranch. Her husband, her one and only true love, was the first person she asked for when she had awakened from the coma. Savannah could count on Bruce to make everything okay for her. He always did. So, when she finally saw her husband walk through the doorway of her hospital room, Savannah reached out to him weakly, palm facing up, and the tears of confusion and terror she had been holding back began to flow unbidden.

"It's okay, Savannah." Bruce quickly dried her tears with a tissue. "I'm here now."

She tried to pull the full-face oxygen mask off, so she could talk to him, to tell him that she loved him, but he stilled her hand by taking it into his and holding on to it firmly.

"You have to get your strength back," Bruce told her.

The mask on her face made her feel claustrophobic, and she wanted to talk. Perhaps her memory was fuzzy about the events that had landed her in the hospital, but she had very distinct memories of her family and Bruce and nurses and doctors all talking around her when she was in the coma. She could hear them murmuring, but no matter how hard she tried to respond, she couldn't. Now that she could talk, she wanted to *talk*.

"I love you," she said, her words muffled by the mask.

Bruce looked at her with an expression she couldn't place. Why didn't he respond right away, as he always had before?

Finally, he squeezed her fingers gently, reassuringly. "I love you."

Behind the mask, her smile was frail, her eyelids slipping downward from exhaustion.

"I'd better let you get some rest." The sound of Bruce's voice made her fight to open her eyes.

When he tried to let go of her hand, she held on, moving her thumb over the empty spot where his wedding band should be.

"Ring?" Her voice was so raspy from having a trachea tube down her throat.

Again, an odd expression flashed in Bruce's sapphire-blue eyes as he glanced down at the ring finger of his left hand.

"It's at home."

"My…ring?"

"I have it," Bruce told her after he dropped a quick kiss on her forehead. "I have your wedding ring."

Retrograde amnesia secondary to traumatic brain injury and stroke. Bottom line, according to Savannah's neurologist: Savannah had lost large swaths of her memory. With time and patience, some, or even all, of her memories could return. Until then…

"What are you suggesting that I do, Carol?" Bruce asked his mother-in-law in a lowered voice. "Move her back to the ranch?"

"We've all tried to talk her into coming home with us, but she wants to be with her husband." Carol's eyes were wide with concern. "She wants to be with you."

Bruce held up his left hand to show Carol his wedding ring. "All she's been talking about for the last two days is getting back into her own bed."

Savannah had been moved to a regular hospital room soon after she had regained consciousness. Her appetite was healthy, she was laughing and talking. Her speech was still a little slurred from the dysarthria, her right hand was a little weak after the ministroke she had sustained, and of course, there was the memory loss. But even with all that, the doctors were getting ready to discharge her and continue with her care as an outpatient. Considering her near-death experience, Savannah was making a quick recovery.

"I know it. I know it." Carol's brows furrowed worriedly. "It's gonna break her sweet heart when she finds out the truth."

They had all hoped that Savannah's memory would return on its own; none of them, including him, wanted to be the one to bring her up to speed on her failed marriage. But her discharge date was barreling toward them with no sign that she had any inkling that they were a signature away from being divorced.

Carol seemed to have something on her mind that she had been skirting ever since he had arrived at the hospital. He had a feeling he knew exactly what his mother-in-law was thinking.

"Would it be such a horrible thing if Savannah moved back to Sugar Creek with you?" she asked him after a couple of silent moments.

Bruce knew it was only a matter of time before Carol asked this question. It was a question that had crossed his own mind a time or two. But it wasn't that simple. Savannah hadn't lived at the ranch with him for a long while. And although he hadn't changed much since she had left, she didn't have clothing or personal items at the ranch.

"Maybe this could be a second chance for the two of you," Carol added.

Carol had always wanted their marriage to work, and had always advocated for spending their attorneys' fees on more marriage counseling.

"You still love her. Even after all that's happened." His mother-in-law looked up into his face hopefully. "Don't you?"

"I'll always love her," he admitted because it was true. And even as angry as he had been with Savannah after all of the fighting and money wasted on attorneys fees, seeing her unconscious in critical care slammed home the truth for him: he still loved her.

Carol's eyes welled with tears. She put her hands on his arm. "And she loves you."

Savannah did love him. Again. It felt bizarre to walk into her hospital room and be greeted with that sweet, welcoming smile he'd first fallen in love with, her hazel-green eyes filled with love and her arms outstretched for a hug. In an odd twist of fate, Savannah was back to being the woman he had married. In an odd twist of fate, Savannah was back in his life.

"Now," Bruce reminded Carol. "She loves me now. What happens when her memory comes back and she remembers that she doesn't love me anymore?"

"I just want to *go home*," Savannah complained to her husband. "I'm so tired of being here. All night long, people are barging into my room, taking my blood pressure, pumping me full of fluids! How can they expect anyone to get better in this place if they won't let us sleep? I'm exhausted, and it's all *their* fault."

When Bruce arrived at the hospital after giving directions to his crew of cowboys at the ranch, Savannah was sitting up in a chair next to her bed.

"Can't you bust me out of this place? I want to sleep in my own bed, with my own pillows." His wife pointed to the small, rectangle pillow on the hospital bed. "*That* horrible thing is a brick disguised as a pillow."

Every time he came to see Savannah in the hospital, she said something that made him laugh. Perhaps that was one of the initial qualities he had liked about her the first time he'd really taken notice of her. She was funny—funnier than any female he'd ever known. And although they had gone to school together virtually all of their lives, they hadn't moved in the same cliques. Savannah had been on the honor roll and sang in the choir and was heavily involved with the school paper and the Beta Club for high achievers.

He'd been the captain of the football team, the popular kid, who happened to be going steady with Kerri Mahoney, the head of the cheerleading squad. He could barely remember seeing her in the halls at school when, as a junior at Montana University conducting research for a bachelor's thesis, Savannah came out to Sugar Creek Ranch looking to study the grazing patterns of their cows. He would never forget how she looked that day—so serious with her round-rimmed glasses, loaded down with an overstuffed computer bag, and the ivory skin of her face devoid of makeup. Savannah hadn't been the least bit interested in him. All of her focus was on his cattle. It had been a rare blow to his ego.

"Let's get you out of this room. Go for a walk."

With one hand, Savannah held on to the rolling stand that held her IV drip, and with the other hand, she held on to his arm. He had to cut his stride in half to make sure that he didn't push her to go faster than her body could handle.

"I feel a breeze on my left butt cheek," Savannah told him. "Take a peek back there for me, will you, and make sure my altogether is altogether covered."

Bruce smiled as he ducked his head back to check out her posterior parts. "You're good."

Halfway down the hall, the pallor of Savannah's oval face turned pasty-white. She swayed against him, and he wrapped his arm around her shoulders.

"Whoa—we've gone far enough for today."

She didn't put up a fight when he helped her make a U-turn so he could take her back to her room. He didn't want to wear her out completely; he still needed to have a serious talk with Savannah. Her doctors were ready to discharge her, and she was ready to leave. If she still wanted to go home to Sugar Creek after he told her the truth about the divorce, he was willing to take her back to the ranch with him. But she had to know the truth. It was her right to know.

He'd already discussed the best way to tell Savannah about the divorce with her doctors and her family. They all agreed that he could tell her privately, but that Carol and John would be on standby in case Savannah needed their emotional support. Bruce had never dreaded a conversation like he dreaded the one he was about to have with his wife. He didn't want to hurt her—even when he had been at his angriest with her, he'd never wanted to hurt her.

After he got her settled back in bed, and the nurses had taken her vital signs and administered medication, Bruce pulled a chair up next to Savannah. He took her hand in his, and it surprised him how easy it was to fall right back into the habit of holding her hand.

"What's bothering you?" Savannah asked him.

Bruce ran his finger over the diamond encrusted platinum wedding band that he had just recently slipped back onto her finger. Savannah didn't remember the day she had taken that ring off and put it on the kitchen counter before she left their home for good. That memory was burned into his brain. He only wished he could erase it. After she'd left, he'd held that ring in his hand for hours, plotting its demise. He thought to throw it away, crush it in the garbage disposal, flush it, melt it down or pawn it. But in the end, he'd thrown it into a dresser drawer, mostly forgotten, until the early-morning hour when Savannah asked about it.

"You've lost a lot of time, Savannah." Bruce started in the only way he knew how.

Fear, fleeting but undeniable, swept over her face. She was scared—scared about the memories she'd lost—and scared that they weren't going to come back.

"Once I get back to my own home, surrounded by all of the things that I love, I really think that it'll all come back." Savannah had an expectant look on her face. "Don't you?"

He wanted to reassure her, but he wasn't as optimistic. She'd lost so much in the accident—it was hard for him to believe that Savannah would ever be exactly as she once was.

"I'd like to think." Bruce tried to take the long way around.

"I just need to go home," she restated. "That's all. I just need to go home."

Still holding on to her hand, Bruce cleared his throat. "Well—that's what I'd like to talk to you about."

With her head resting on the pillow, her dark brown hair fanned out around her face, her eyes intent on him, Savannah waited for him to continue.

"There's a lot that's gone on between us, Savannah. A lot that you don't remember."

Savannah's fingers tightened around his fingers, that look of fear and discomfort back in her eyes. "You're scaring me."

He didn't want to scare her—and he told her as much.

"Just tell me what's on your mind, Bruce."

Her entreaty was faint and laced with uneasiness. Savannah had always been a "pull the Band-Aid off quick" kind of person. She didn't like to draw things out.

Bruce had spent the last two years fighting like cats and dogs with this woman, and now all he wanted to do was protect her from the pain they had willingly caused each other. He dropped his head for a moment and shook it. The only way out was forward.

"For the last couple of years, we've been going through a divorce," Bruce finally mustered the guts to tell her. The sound of her sharp intake of breath brought his eyes back to hers. The look in her eyes could only be described as stunned.

Savannah looked down at their hands, at their wedding rings. She swallowed several times, her eyes filling with unshed tears, before she asked, "You weren't wearing your ring. When I first saw you. You weren't wearing it. Are we even…married?"

He held on to her hand even though it seemed as

if she were already trying to pull it away. How many times had he wished for a second chance with Savannah? He hadn't wanted it this way—never this way— but he would be a fool to let her slip away from him a second time without putting up one heck of a fight.

"We're still married," he reassured her. It wasn't important, right at this moment, for Savannah to know just how close they had come to ending their marriage.

"I don't remember…" Savannah stopped midsentence, tears slipping unchecked onto her cheeks.

"It's going to be okay, Savannah." He felt impotent to console her. There weren't words that could make this right for her.

Savannah stared at him hard, with a look of distrust in her eyes. "How can you *say* that? We've split up, but it's going to be fine? Why would you want a divorce? What happened to us?"

When he didn't answer right away, she tugged her fingers loose from his hold.

"Tell me why."

How could he explain the last several years of their marriage in a sentence or two? There were things that they had all agreed that Savannah didn't need to know right now.

"I didn't file for divorce, Savannah. You did."

Bewildered, she stared into his eyes, seeming to be searching for answers. "I did? Why? Why would I do that?"

"We had a lot of problems we just couldn't seem to work out," he told her honestly.

Savannah covered her face with her hands. In a muffled voice, she said, "I just want to go home."

Bruce moved to her side; sitting on the edge of

the bed, he pulled her hands down from her face and tugged her gently into his arms so he could comfort her in the only way he knew how. He ran his hand over the back of her hair, the way she always liked him to do, and was relieved that, instead of drawing away from him, Savannah leaned against him and rested her head on his shoulder.

"Come home to me, Savannah." Bruce hugged his wife, his eyes closed.

Savannah broke the embrace and studied his face, looking directly into his eyes again when she asked him, "Do you still love me?"

The cowboy answered firmly and without any hesitation, "Yes, Beautiful. Yes, I do."

Chapter Two

"So, this is over." Kerri had been sitting across from him at her small kitchen table, not saying a word, arms crossed in front of her body.

Bruce sat stiffly in the chair opposite Kerri. He'd never felt truly comfortable at Kerri's table—the chairs were too small, the table too low. Today, he felt uncomfortable for a whole new set of reasons.

"I'm sorry." He apologized for the second time. His apology may have sounded hollow to Kerri's ears, but it was sincere. If he'd known that he had even a fraction of a shot of winning Savannah back, he'd never have rekindled his old high school romance with Kerri. He wasn't in the business of breaking hearts for the fun of it.

"You're sorry." Kerri made a little sarcastic laugh as

she looked out the kitchen window. "Well, that makes it all better then, doesn't it?"

Bruce stared at the woman he'd cared about for most of his life. Her forgiveness could be a long time coming.

Bruce stood up and grabbed his hat off the table. "I'd better go."

Kerri didn't look at him. She gave a small, annoyed shake of her head, but she refused to look at him even as he opened the door to leave.

"If you ever need me, I'm just a phone call away." Bruce paused in the entranceway, the door half-open.

Kerri hadn't said a word, hadn't looked his way once, and there were tears flowing freely onto her cheek.

"Take care of yourself," Bruce said before he ducked out of the door, choked up at the sight of Kerri's tears. He cared an awful lot about Kerri. He always had. But Savannah was his heart.

"Home!" Savannah exclaimed as she walked through the back door of the modest log cabin they had designed and built together. "I'm finally *home*!"

Bruce had never thought to hear those words come out of his wife's mouth again. He followed her into the mudroom, carrying in each hand two heavy suitcases packed by her family. They were greeted by three dogs, mutts all, tails wagging, barking excitedly. Savannah immediately fell to her knees and hugged the large dogs around their necks, calling two of the dogs by name, and laughing as the rescue mutts knocked her backward while fighting for the chance to lick her on the face.

Bruce dropped the suitcases with a loud thud so he could intervene. "Whoa, sit, boys!"

"I'm okay." Savannah reassured him, now sitting cross-legged on the wood floor, her arms still wrapped around Buckley's furry neck. "I've missed you guys so much!"

Savannah had never shied away from the dogs giving her a tongue bath on her face, not since the first day she had come out to Sugar Creek. Bruce decided to join in on the reunion instead of trying to control it. He rubbed Buckley between the ears, his favorite spot, while Savannah showed some individual love and attention to Murphy.

With a happy laugh, Savannah turned her attention to the dog he had rescued off the side of the road. "And who are you?"

"That's Hound Dog."

"It's nice to meet you, Hound Dog." His wife smiled at the tan-and-black dog with long floppy ears before she turned her eyes his way. "How long have we had him?"

Bruce stood up and held out his hand to help his wife onto her feet.

"I haven't had him for all that long. Six months, maybe. Found him on the side of I-90, dehydrated, half-starved. An infection in one of his paws so bad the vet thought we might have to amputate."

Bruce rubbed Hound Dog's head. "It shows you what a little love can do."

Savannah gazed up at him with an appreciative look in her eyes. She tucked her hand under his arm and leaned into his side. "You've never been able to ignore an animal in need."

Instinctively, his body tensed. Yes, he had become used to holding Savannah's hand in the hospital, and, yes, he still loved her. But he was having a difficult time accepting all of those little intimate touches that were a part of married life. It had been years since Savannah wanted to touch him; post-accident, Savannah seemed to want to touch him all the time, like she had when they were first married. It was unnerving.

Bruce tried not to be obvious when he took a step away from her. "Let's get you settled."

Once in the master bedroom, he hoisted the two suitcases, one at a time, onto their queen bed. Savannah had opened the door to the cedar-lined walk-in closet and strode inside. He found her standing in the center of the closet, quietly staring at all of the empty rods and shoe racks on what had been her side of the closet.

"Everything okay?"

The color had drained from her face; her arms were crossed tightly in front of her body. Her slender shoulders were slumped forward, and she seemed to be emotionally swallowed up much in the same way her torso was swallowed up by the sweatshirt she had insisted on wearing home. "I really left."

It was a statement, even though there was a question in her voice. She wanted to know what had happened—she wanted to know why she had left. But they had all agreed—her doctors, her family—that it would be better on Savannah to wait a couple of weeks before that subject was broached.

"Hey." Bruce wanted to distract her before she started to ask the next inevitable questions. "Why don't we tackle this later? I'm starved. How 'bout you?"

Savannah shrugged noncommittally. "If you're hungry, I'll try to eat."

Bruce held out his hand to his wife, palm facing up. After a moment, Savannah shut off the closet light and slipped her hand into his. At least for now, he had diverted her from the inevitable conversation about the reason behind their split. For now, he had his wife back.

Her first night out of the hospital was a strange mixture of joy, relief, confusion and discomfort. As much as Bruce tried to act "normal" around her, his body language didn't lie. He felt uncomfortable having her back in the home, and she knew it by the little nervous laugh he would make after trying to explain the changes in their home. At first glance, the house had seemed the same. But after the initial blast of relief subsided, Savannah started to notice little differences. She loved to collect refrigerator magnets, and all of her magnets were gone from the simple black refrigerator in their galley kitchen. Her favorite "chicken and egg" salt and pepper shakers she had picked up in a yard sale had been replaced with generic shakers from the grocery store. How could all of those little touches make such a big difference in the feel of the home? It was as if she had been deliberately erased.

For a moment, she closed her eyes, pushing back a wave of sadness. What a cruel trick, this head injury. She could remember the early part of their married lives together, but couldn't remember what led them to separate. She couldn't remember ever being apart from Bruce. It was so…unfair.

"D'you get enough to eat?" Bruce broke her train of thought.

Savannah opened her eyes and put her hand on the spot on the fireplace mantel where their mismatched compilation of family photos had once been kept. She nodded her head, not turning to face him. Suddenly, the excitement of being home and the realization, if not the actual memory, that she had left the home she had built and loved, struck her like another blow to her head. Her fingers tightened on the rough-hewn mantel that Bruce had crafted by hand; she felt herself sway and the room began to spin.

"Whoa!" She heard Bruce's deep voice, felt his large, warm hand on her elbow to steady her. "What happened?"

Savannah closed her eyes and swallowed back the feeling of nausea. "My head is killing me."

"We overdid it."

"Yes." Her response was weak, more from sadness than loss of strength.

Bruce put his arm around her shoulder for support. "Let's get you to bed."

She nodded her agreement. Bed was exactly what she needed. She wanted to snuggle down into her own bed, with her own mattress and pillows, and pull the comforter up over her head so she could shut the world out for a bit. Savannah left Bruce and the dogs in the bedroom while she got ready for bed in the bathroom. She had never shut the door on her husband before when she moved through her nightly routine, yet tonight felt different.

"Let me know if you need anything," Bruce told her through the closed door.

"Okay," she said after she spit toothpaste into the sink.

After she was done digging out her toiletries from her small carry-on bag, Savannah sat on the edge of the tub and stared at her reflection in the mirror. She tried to tuck her longish bangs behind her ear so she could lightly touch the large, rectangular bandage on her forehead. The right side of her face was still puffy with green-and-yellow bruising around her right eye and cheek. Small cuts and scratches on her nose and chin, already on their way to healing, had scabbed over. In her opinion, she looked like a hot mess, but not just because of the bruises and scratches and bandage. She didn't like her hair at all; sometime during the lost years, she had decided to go with bangs, blond streaks and layers. Three of her most hated hairstyle don'ts! What had possessed her to do that? It looked *awful*.

After a long inhale and exhale, Savannah pulled a face before she stood up cautiously and opened the bathroom door. In her favorite flannel long-sleeved pajamas, she faced the four males in her life. Buck and Hound Dog had already staked out their spots on the bed, while Murphy, the dog that had always favored her, was waiting patiently just on the other side of the bathroom threshold. Bruce was standing on the far side of the bed—her side of the bed—waiting for her. He seemed awkward and stiff to her, and there was a concerned look in his striking blue eyes.

She spoke to the concern she saw in his eyes as she bent down to pet Murphy on the head. "I'm okay. Just really tired."

Bruce had pulled the sheets and comforter back so she could easily slide into bed. As she walked by him, he held his body stiff and away from her. Her husband gave her a dose of her medicine, redressed the bandage on her head and then pulled the covers up to her chest after she lay back on the pillows.

"I haven't been tucked into bed since I was a kid," she mused, her eyes intent on Bruce's face.

"I won't do it anymore if it bothers you." Bruce switched off the light on the nightstand.

"No," she said faintly. "It makes me feel..."

Loved by you, cared for by you—

"Safe," she finished after a pause.

In the low light from the hallway, Savannah saw the smallest of smiles drift across Bruce's handsome face.

"Sleep well." He turned away from the bed.

Savannah had slipped her hand out from beneath the comforter to catch his hand.

"I love you." They had never gone to bed without telling each other that they loved each other—not that she could remember, anyway. It had been their promise to each other—never go to bed mad. Never go to bed without saying "I love you."

Bruce turned back to her, his eyes so intent on her face. After a squeeze of her fingers, Bruce replied, "I love you more."

After tucking Savannah into bed, Bruce went through the motions of cleaning up the kitchen, starting the dishwasher and letting the dogs out one last time. Normally, his three canine companions would stick to his side like glue, following him from room to room. Tonight was different. All three dogs opted to return to the bedroom, to get back into bed with Savannah. He'd felt so lonely after Savannah had left him, that he often found any reason not to be inside the house until he was ready to fall into bed. And he had counted on the dogs to fill some of the void left by his wife.

Now, sitting on the couch in the living room, the only light provided by the three-quarter moon glowing in the purple-black sky, Bruce felt more alone than ever. Having Savannah's energy back in the house, when he thought to never have it back, had been more of a shock to his system than he had expected. Even though it had felt like the heart had been hollowed out of the house, he supposed he had grown accustomed to it.

He hadn't discussed the sleeping arrangements with Savannah—he assumed that she understood that they wouldn't be sharing a bed. He'd turned the second bedroom into a storage room, so his only option was the couch. He had moved his necessary toiletries into the spare bathroom, and that was where he prepared for bed. Wearing only his gray boxer briefs, Bruce lay back on the couch, stuffing two of the couch pillows beneath his head. With a tired sigh, he pulled the blanket draped over the back of the sofa down over his torso. The blanket smelled strongly of wet dog; Bruce pushed the blanket down to cover his groin, and far enough away from his nose not to be distracted by the smell. He'd wash the blanket tomorrow.

Arm behind his head, the cowboy stared up at the vaulted ceiling of the log cabin, his mind racing with "what if" scenarios revolving around Savannah and her missing memories. It was a good long while before he could finally close his eyes and fall into a fitful sleep. But this sleep, as restless as it was, didn't last long. At first, he thought that he had dreamed the sound of dogs barking in the distance; it wasn't until he felt a dog licking him on the side of his face and mouth that he began to awaken.

"What?" Bruce asked Murphy as he sat up while at the same time wiping his hand over his mouth to clean away the dog's saliva.

Murphy disappeared back into the bedroom and joined the other two dogs barking. Bruce stood up, expecting to go tell the dogs to be quiet so they wouldn't awaken Savannah, but then his wife cried out, the words muffled by the barking.

"Savannah!" Bruce rushed to his wife's side.

"Can you hear me! Can you hear me!" Savannah was sitting up in bed, crying, her head in her hands. "*Why* can't you hear me!"

Bruce switched on the light near the bed, and guided the dogs away from Savannah so he could sit down next to her on the bed.

"Hey." He made her lift her head so he could see her face. She looked terrified, sweat mingled with tears on her flushed cheeks, her eyes wide.

Still crying, Savannah lurched forward and wrapped her arms around his body. "I was screaming and screaming and screaming and no one could hear me. Not you, not Mom, not Dad. *No one.*"

Bruce rested his head on the top of hers and let her cry it out on his shoulder. "You're safe, Savannah. It was just a bad dream."

After she took a couple of deep, steadying breaths, he leaned back so he could see her face. Bruce brushed the sweat-dampened hair off his wife's forehead, then held her face gently in his hands and wiped her tears away with his thumbs.

"Please, stop calling me Savannah," his wife said,

her face crumpling as if she were about to start crying again.

Savannah pulled back from him a little; he dropped his hands from her face.

"You only call me Savannah when we fight," she added when he didn't respond right away.

It was true—he called her "Beautiful." He had rarely used her first name during their courtship and their marriage. But for the last year, he'd called her Savannah exclusively.

"All right," he agreed. What else could he do but agree?

Savannah went to the restroom while he went to the kitchen to get her a glass of water. When he returned, his wife was back in bed surrounded by his traitorous canines.

"Guys, you need to get down," Bruce said to the dogs. Savannah barely had enough room to sleep.

"No," Savannah said quickly, almost dribbling her sip of water. "I want them here."

At this moment, he would have granted Savannah just about anything. He hated to see her cry—it broke his heart when she cried.

He waited while Savannah finished the glass of water; he took the empty glass. "Better?"

She nodded, pulling on a loose thread in the pattern of the comforter. After a minute, she looked up at him. "Where were you?"

Bruce was about to switch off the light again, but straightened instead. He sent Savannah a questioning gaze.

"When I woke up, you weren't in bed." Her eyes

slid over to the undisturbed pillows and comforter on his side of the bed.

They hadn't discussed the sleeping arrangement— she hadn't brought it up and neither had he. Perhaps it was sheer cowardice that had stopped him from broaching the subject; he figured that Savannah would assume that he would be sharing their marital bed as usual. He'd known all along that he intended to sleep on the couch.

Bruce swallowed hard and pushed his hair back off his face. "I think I should sleep on the couch for a while."

Savannah couldn't hide the hurt she felt, and he closed his eyes for a split second to block out the pain he could see in her eyes before he continued. "I know this is hard for you, Savannah,"

She had dropped her eyes, but raised them when he used her first name.

"Beautiful," he corrected. "I'm sorry. I just need a minute to—" he paused, his forehead wrinkled with his own pain "—adjust."

They said good-night for the second time that night; the three dogs stayed faithfully with Savannah while he returned, alone, to the couch and the smelly blanket. If their first night was any indication of how difficult it was going to be to have Savannah back at Sugar Creek Ranch, it promised to be a tough row to hoe— for the both of them.

Chapter Three

"Well, where the hell is she?" Jock Brand demanded. "Why the hell didn't you bring her with you?"

Bruce arrived at Sugar Creek's traditional Sunday brunch without Savannah, much to the unabashed displeasure of his father.

As Jock's eldest of eight children from two marriages, Bruce had learned to ignore most of his father's bluster and salty language long ago. He leaned down to kiss his stepmother, Lilly, on her soft, light brown cheek, before taking his seat at the long formal dining table.

"I let her sleep in," Bruce told his father. "She needs the rest."

He didn't add that he didn't want Savannah to feel overwhelmed by his family right off the bat; Sunday brunch was the one time when they converged on the ranch. And when the talk turned to politics, as it often did, yelling and fist-banging on the table were as common a fare as eggs and bacon.

"A hearty breakfast and hard work," Jock countered loudly. "That's what she needs."

Jock never used an "indoor voice," and his answer for all things was a good breakfast followed by hard work. And Bruce had to acknowledge that his father led by that example. Jock wasn't a man known for his kindness or his forgiving nature, but he was known for throwing his back into every aspect of his life. Years of working in the harsh elements of Montana were carved into his narrow face by deep wrinkles fanning out from his eyes and crisscrossing his broad forehead. His nose was prominent, strong and slightly crooked, with a hump in the middle from a break that hadn't been set properly. His hair, thin and receding at the temples, had long since turned white, as had the bushy, unruly eyebrows framing the deeply set, sapphire-blue eyes. At one time, Jock's skin had been fair, but decades of work in the sun without any sun protection had given his leathery skin a brownish-ruddy hue.

"She needs her rest," Lilly said in her soft, steady voice as she poured coffee into the cup at Bruce's place setting.

Lilly was Jock's second wife, and the entire family still marveled at the match. Jock was loud and abrasive; Lilly was quiet and sweet. Jock believed in "spare the rod, spoil the child;" Lilly believed in the power of kind words and affection. Jock was a sworn atheist; Lilly, on the other hand, was a very spiritual woman with a deep connection to the land. A full-blooded Chippewa-Cree Native American raised on the Rocky Boy reservation, Lilly Hanging Cloud was an undeniable beauty—kind brown-black eyes, balanced, even features and prominent cheekbones. Her hair, always worn long and straight, was coal black with silver laced throughout. Yes, Lilly was his stepmother, but his memory of his own mother was so faint that Lilly was truly the only mother he'd ever known.

"Morning!" Jessie, Jock's only daughter and the youngest of the bunch, breezed into the dining room, her waist-length, pin-straight raven hair fluttering behind her. Their baby sister was sweet, but had been spoiled by all of them, including him. She had always been too adorable to scold, with her mother's striking features and her father's shocking blue eyes.

Now that Jessie was here, Jock's attention would turn to his favored child, and Bruce would be able to eat in peace for a moment or two.

"Hi, Daddy." Jessie leaned down and kissed their father's cheek; she was the only one of his eight children who got away with calling him "Daddy." All of the siblings, including him, called the patriarch of their family "Jock" or "sir."

Jessie then kissed her mother "good morning," plopped down in the chair next to him and bumped her shoulder into his. "Hi, dork."

Bruce wrapped his arm around his sister's shoulder, pulled her close for a moment and kissed the side of her head. "Mornin', brat."

A steady trickle of Brand siblings filled the empty seats at the enormous dining table. One of his full brothers, Liam, was the first to arrive, followed by their half brothers Colton and Hunter. Shane and Gabe, his other two full-blooded brothers, were missing from breakfast, as was his youngest half brother, Noah. Gabe, a long-distance trucker, was out of town, and no one expected Shane to show. Shane was honorably discharged from the army; diagnosed with PTSD, he was often missing from family events. Noah, a private first class in the Marine Corps, had been recently deployed to South Korea.

As the long dining table filled with his children, Jock presided over Sunday breakfast like a king over his court. Bruce was happy to drift into the background while his siblings dominated the conversation, each one louder than the other, trying as they always did to get the loudest and the last word on all subjects. They were a competitive bunch—but tight as family could be when push came to shove. When the conversation, as it often did, turned to politics, Bruce found his thoughts returning to his wife. The shock of her coming back to Sugar Creek Ranch hadn't worn off; he knew that she must feel the distance between them. He could read the pain in her eyes when he avoided touching her or stiffened when she innocently placed her hand over his. He wanted to open his heart to her again, but he couldn't. Not yet. The first time she'd walked out of his life and into the arms of another man, it had left him feeling like an empty eggshell—cracked, fragile and good for nothing. He had to protect his heart. What other choice did he have?

"Savannah!" his sister screamed over the din of voices.

Everyone at the table stopped talking and turned their attention to the entrance to the dining room.

Bruce had caught the expression on his sister's face, lit up with happy surprise, before he turned his head to look at the doorway to the dining room. Savannah, her slender body engulfed in one of his denim button-down shirts, was standing in the doorway appearing peaked and frail. She had an uncertainty in her body language, a nervousness in her half smile and forward-slumped shoulders that Bruce read right away. Savannah knew in her mind that she had been absent from Sunday breakfast for a long time; it would be normal to wonder about how the family would receive her. And she had some reason to be concerned—several of his siblings were still raw with Savannah and her lawyer, so they weren't ready to welcome her back to the fold with open arms. Their father had no such reservations.

"Daughter!" Jock bellowed as he thrust his seat back and out of his way so he could wrap a possessive, welcoming arm around Savannah's shoulders. Sugar Creek was Jock's ranch—if he said Savannah was welcome, she *was* welcome.

"Good morning, everyone," Savannah said with an unusually shy smile and a quieter than normal voice. She leaned into her father-in-law's embrace, but her eyes had sought out his.

Bruce had stood up at the same time as his father; it was instinctive, natural, to protect his wife—to stand between her and her critics in the room. Even if those critics were his own kin.

"You need something to eat," Lilly observed.

Before his wife could respond, Jock waved his hand over the table. "Everyone move. *Move!* I want Savannah to sit down right here next to me."

"No, don't do that..." Savannah tried to intervene, but Jock's will was the will of the family.

Everyone on the right side of the table, including

him, moved one seat down to make room for their father's most-favored daughter-in-law.

Bruce had gathered up his dishes, swapped them for a clean set and held the chair for his wife to sit down.

"Sorry." Savannah apologized to the table at large.

"Don't you go apologizing for nothing," Jock ordered gruffly. "It's been far too long since we've had you at this table."

The mood at the table changed; the conversation seemed stilted and stiff to Bruce, with his siblings focusing more on their food than talking. Savannah, who used to be a ray of sun shining on Sunday breakfast, had now become a bit of a spoiler. One by one, his brothers finished their meals and dispersed. Liam, his junior by only one year and always the peacemaker, made sure to say a kind word to Savannah, wishing her a speedy recovery, before he left. Jessie was the only sibling who seemed to have made a seamless pivot now that the divorce was on hold; she talked in a stream of consciousness, bouncing from one topic to another, seeming to want to catch Savannah up on the missing years in one sitting.

"Come up for air," Bruce told his sister. "She's not going anywhere."

Had he just spoken the truth? The truth from somewhere deep inside? Or was that hopeful thinking?

Instead of making a quick appearance at breakfast as he had planned, Bruce sat beside his wife while she ate two full helpings of scrambled eggs, a heaping scoop of cheese grits, a biscuit slathered with butter and honey, and drank a large glass of freshly squeezed orange juice. He'd never known her to be much of a breakfast person.

"I'm stuffed." Savannah groaned, her hands on her stomach.

"You sure you can't eat a few more spoonfuls of grits?" Bruce teased her. "I'd hate for those couple of bites to go to waste."

Savannah pushed her plate away and scrunched up her face distastefully. "I may not eat for the rest of the day."

"I haven't seen you eat that much in a day before," Bruce mused.

"A hearty breakfast is exactly what you needed." Jock gave a nod of approval.

Rosario, the house manager for years, and one of her subordinates, Donna, came into the dining room to begin clearing the table.

"Breakfast was good?" Rosario asked, her hand affectionately on Jock's shoulder, while Donna began to clear. Rosario had been with the family for decades, and the house manager had long since become more family than employee.

"It was damn good." Jock tossed his crumpled napkin onto his plate.

"I'm glad." The house manager's eyes crinkled deeply at the corner when she smiled. "It's good to see you at the table again, Miss Savannah."

Savannah placed her neatly folded napkin on top of her empty plate. "It's good to be seen, Rosario."

"We all missed you," Donna said as she reached around in front of Savannah to get her plate.

"Oh…" his wife said, and he could tell by the confused look in her eyes that the memory of Donna had been ripped away, like so many others, by the crash. "Thank you."

"I think I'd like to go home and rest now." Savannah put her hand on his arm.

Bruce gave her a nod of understanding; he said, as he pushed back his chair, "You outdid yourselves as usual, ladies."

Savannah gave Jock a hug and a kiss, said goodbye to everyone in the room, and then, arms crossed in front of her body, she walked into the grand, circular, three-story foyer.

"Hold up." Jock stood up so he could say what he intended to say in a lowered voice.

Bruce waited for his father's next words; the patriarch made a little motion near his mouth. "She sounds kinda funny when she talks. You gonna get that fixed?"

"It's in the works. We're just waiting for insurance to shuffle things around. I'm hoping to get her to therapy starting next week."

Jock gave a nod of understanding accompanied by a single pat on the shoulder.

Savannah was waiting for him on the wide porch that ran the length of the expansive main house. She was sitting on the top step of the wood stairs with their three canines gathered around her; she was staring out at the fields in the distance with the slow-moving herd of cows as they grazed in the early-afternoon sun.

Bruce knelt down so he could greet the dogs. "You all right?"

It took her a couple of seconds to nod "yes," but he didn't believe it. The breakfast had rattled her; being with his family had rattled her.

Her body was curled forward like a turtle shell; it seemed to him like she was trying to disappear into his shirt. Acting, not thinking, Bruce held out his hand to his wife.

"Come on," he said gently. "Let's get you back to bed."

Savannah had turned her head away from him; when she turned it back, there were tears clinging to her eyelashes. She lowered her head and wiped the tears on the sleeve of her borrowed shirt.

"I don't want to go back to bed," she finally said.

Bruce looked down into her face—a face he had both loved and resented. "What do you want to do, then?"

"I don't know." Savannah's eyes returned to the horizon, her arms locked around Hound Dog's thick neck for comfort. "Sunday was always *our* day."

Bruce stood up to full height and slid his hands into his front pockets. Sunday had always been their day—a day they reserved for their relationship. But that had been a long time ago.

"When's the last time we spent a Sunday together?" she asked him without looking at him.

With a frown, Bruce answered her honestly. "I can't remember the last time."

Savannah gave a little sad shake of her head. "For me, it was just last week."

Her husband had offered to stay with her—to reboot their Sunday tradition. But it felt forced to her, so she declined. Bruce had a list of chores he had planned for his Sunday, and she didn't want to keep him from his work. Murphy and Buckley followed behind her husband; Hound Dog stayed with her. Perhaps he sensed that she was new to the dog pack, like he was. She was grateful for the company, now that she was feeling, for the first time, like a stranger in her own home.

Her sisters had always been her solace, so she called her youngest sister, Joy, who had returned to Nashville, Tennessee where she was attending graduate school at Vanderbilt University.

"It was terrible," she recounted for her sister. "Everyone stopped talking when I walked in, half of his brothers looked at me like I'd grown devil horns and a tail—they *hate* me now—*and* I didn't recognize this lady, Donna, who works there who obviously knows me. I felt so nervous that I ate enough food to feed a small army…"

"I'm sorry, Savannah." Her sister, Joy, said in a sympathetic tone. "It's like a bad dream."

Savannah was standing by the picture window, watching Bruce unload wood from the back of his truck and carry it to his workshop.

"It *was* like a bad dream," she said of the breakfast. "Like that dream when you wake up late and you rush to work and everyone is staring at you like you're a freak, and then you realize that you're naked."

"I've never had that dream before."

"Well, I have. It's the worst." She sat down on the couch with Hound Dog faithfully parked at her feet.

Savannah sighed, noticing that her head was throbbing again. "I don't know, Joy. I didn't know it was going to be this way. I don't know what I was expecting…"

"For things to be normal."

She shrugged one shoulder. "Yeah. I guess so."

After a silent moment, her sister probed. "Do you

still think you're ready to find out why the marriage fell apart?"

Before she had left the hospital, she had argued with her family about just this topic. She had been so *certain* that she could handle anything that she found out about her marriage. But now? One awkward breakfast had made her feel so depressed, so disconnected from the Brand family. She used to be a favored sister to Bruce's brothers. Now, the way Gabe and Hunter had looked at her…

Joy added when her sister didn't respond right away, "If you want me to tell you what happened, Savannah, you know I will."

"No," Savannah said with a definitive shake of the head. "I'm not ready. Not yet."

She had sulked for a while after she had placed calls to both sisters and her mother. But then Savannah decided that moping wasn't her idea of making use of a beautiful Sunday. She found her way out to a patch of ground that was her kitchen garden; she loved to cook with fresh, homegrown vegetables picked right out of the garden. The garden was overgrown with layers of weeds; the pretty little white picket fence Bruce had built and painted as a surprise for her was dirty and unkempt. With her hands on her hips, Savannah shook her head. The fence, once her pride, was leaning in places; pickets were broken from animals and weather.

"What a mess."

The garden seemed to be a metaphor for her marriage. Would she ever get used to seeing things so changed, when in her mind, it was just yesterday when her life was perfect? Her marriage had been full of laughter and romance and lovemaking; she'd been a beloved member of Sugar Creek Ranch and her garden had been teeming with fresh veggies, ripe for the picking.

"How do you eat an elephant, Hound Dog?" she asked her companion.

She was going to clean up this garden, one weed at a time. Savannah found her toolshed virtually untouched; she pulled on her gloves, and retrieved hand tools and a sturdy hoe. Armed with her weapons to beat back the weeds and decay, she stepped into the garden, reclaimed the ground as her own, dropped to her knees and began to yank out the weeds. A couple of weeds into the process, sweat began to form on her forehead and on her neck. It felt good to sweat; it felt good to take out her frustration on these stupid, creeping weeds that had ruined her beautiful garden.

"What are you doing?"

Savannah had been deep in thought, focused on ripping as many weeds from the ground as possible; she hadn't heard her husband approach. She sat back on her heels and wiped the sweat from her brow before it rolled down into her eyes.

"Pulling weeds."

Bruce—to her, the most handsome man in the world—had his shirt unbuttoned and his stomach, chest and neck were covered in sweat. Normally—at least the normal she remembered—she would have stood up and wiped that sweat from his neck and chest with her hands, stealing a kiss along the way. It hadn't taken her long at all to figure out that this sexual flirtation wouldn't be welcome. Not long at all.

"You have a concussion, Savannah," he reminded her in a slightly condescending way.

She stared at him in response.

He added, a little less bossy, "The doctor said you needed to rest."

"*This is* how I rest," Savannah argued. She turned back to her weeds. "If I go to bed now, I'll be awake all night. You know that's true."

Silence stretched out between them, and then she heard him walk away. She didn't glance behind her to watch him; she focused on the blasted weeds instead. She hadn't expected him to join her—they didn't spend Sundays together anymore. And yet, he did return. Wordlessly, Bruce came back to the garden with Buckley and Murphy following at his heels. He knelt down in the dirt and began to pull out the weeds in the second row.

They worked like that silently, side by side, until they had completely cleared the first two rows of her garden of the layers of overgrowth. Bruce stood up and then offered his hand to her, which she accepted. Toward the end of the row, she was beginning to feel exhausted and woozy. But she was determined to finish at least one row before she gave in to her body.

"Well," Savannah said, more to herself than to Bruce. "It's a start."

Bruce was staring at her face with an inscrutable expression in his slightly narrowed, bright blue eyes. "Yes," he agreed after a moment. "I suppose it is."

Chapter Four

During the first week that Savannah was back at the ranch, Bruce watched her slowly, day by day, reclaim their log cabin as her own. She had unearthed their framed wedding pictures in one of the drawers in the living room and put them back in their original spot on the fireplace mantel. One of her antique bud vases, a least favorite that she had left behind, was back on the kitchen windowsill with a sprig of wildflowers soaking in the morning sun. The more his wife settled back into their marital home, the more accustomed to sharing the space Bruce became.

He was becoming accustomed to having Savannah's toothbrush, face creams, perfumes and deodorant on the bathroom counter next to his small array of toiletries; he was becoming accustomed to the sound of music playing when he arrived home. It was good to have music back in the house.

"Smells good in here." Bruce hung his cowboy hat on the hook inside of the door.

Today his wife was in the mood for Fleetwood Mac.

Savannah appeared from the kitchen, surprised by his early arrival.

"I wasn't expecting you until later," she said with a small smile, wiping her hands on a dish towel.

Bruce walked the whole way to her side; he had been trying to open up more to Savannah. She had, understandably, pulled away from him once she began to live the truth of their separation, even when her brain wouldn't remember. So they stood, rather awkwardly, a foot apart, without kissing each other in greeting as they always had.

"I decided to knock off a little early today." He leaned down to pet Hound Dog, who was now glued to Savannah's side.

She nodded wordlessly, her smile not completely reaching her eyes.

"What's cooking?"

Now her smile widened. "Guess!"

Bruce played along, looking upward in thought. "It's not… Buffalo Pockets?"

Beef, assorted vegetables and seasonings baked in foil pockets. One of his favorite meals—easy, hardy, but so damn good.

"I wanted to say thank-you—for helping me with the garden." Savannah turned to walk back to the kitchen.

Hound Dog left him and followed behind her.

He wasn't sure how to respond. How many times had he looked out at that garden feeling guilty about letting the elements and the wild animals have their way with it? Savannah had loved that garden, and it was one way, a petty way, to strike back at her.

"I'm gonna clean up," Bruce told her. "For dinner."

On the way into the bedroom, the bedroom he hadn't slept in since Savannah's return, he picked up a pair of socks and a pair of boots—she had never been able to get her clothes in the hamper or her shoes back in the closet. She often just left her clothes where she stripped out of them; it had always annoyed him, and perhaps it still did, but not with the same force as before. How many times had he missed her jeans on the floor after she left? Many times.

What Savannah lacked in housekeeping motivation, she made up for tenfold when it came to cooking. Man, had he missed his wife's cooking, and he told her so.

The good smells emanating from the kitchen had gotten him to speed up his shower, get dressed quick, so he could take his seat at their kitchen table. While Savannah had been gone, this table had been used as a catchall for the mail and any junk he accumulated in his pockets during his workday.

"I love cooking for you." Savannah smiled at him sweetly as she collected his empty plate.

"That was one hell of a good meal, Beautiful." He leaned back, feeling stuffed after two heaping servings. Bruce had been subsisting on frozen meals for a year. Yes, he could have had dinner at the main house, but his father's loud and consistent disapproval over his divorce had deterred him pretty quickly.

"I hope you left some room for dessert," Savannah said as she carried their dishes the short distance to the kitchen. "Lilly and I stopped off at the bakery on the way home."

Bruce followed her to the kitchen, his hands full with as many items as he could carry. Jock had never once helped wife one or wife two in the kitchen, but Bruce had always considered it to be part of marriage. It had always been those little things, like Savannah cooking while he did the dishes, that had made him want to be a married man. And for a while there, he had managed to have a perfect marriage, to the perfect woman for him. For a while there, he had managed to marry his best friend.

"All I have to do is pop them in the oven." Savannah held up a plate of raspberry chocolate turnovers, freshly made from his favorite bakery.

Bruce filled the sink with water and soap and set the dishes in the hot, sudsy water to soak. He wiped his hands off on a dish towel, his mouth watering for the tangy, sweet dessert, but his stomach needed a little extra room before the next course.

He smiled his thank-you. "You know what I love."

Bruce saw a pretty flush of color on his wife's cheeks before she turned away to put the plate on the counter. "Should I heat the oven now? Or wait?"

It had been such a long time since he wanted to pull Savannah into his arms and kiss her. But, oh, how he wanted to kiss her right at that moment. The kindness of her gesture, the sweet blush on her cheeks that spoke of her ability to have a reaction to being in close quarters with him. He felt her attraction for him, just as strong as when they were first married. And in turn, his body, his mind, his heart, were all reacting.

"You up for a walk?" he asked her, not at all sure

that she would accept. Nothing was certain with Savannah. With a nod to the plate of pastries, he added, "I need to make some room for at least three of those."

Walking after dinner had been one of their marriage staples; they both loved to walk in the evening with the dogs, hoping to catch a colorful sunset. Even the rain hadn't deterred their evening routine; they had just grabbed raincoats and gone.

Bruce held the door open for his wife, and then grabbed his hat off the rack as he stepped out onto the porch. As usual, the dogs happily mobbed Savannah, who greeted them as if she hadn't seen them in days, not just an hour.

"Which way?" she asked at the bottom of the steps.

"Cook's choice."

They headed toward the west, toward the setting sun and toward one of the many pastures where some of the herd of black Angus were lying down after a day of grazing. They would have held hands—they always had—but this time, she didn't reach for his hand, and he couldn't bring himself to reach for hers.

Silently, they walked together, side by side, until they reached the pasture fence. With a sigh, Savannah leaned on the fence to admire the view. Perhaps he was biased—most likely he was—but Sugar Creek Ranch was heaven on Earth. A landscape seemingly touched by God's hand, it featured flat pastureland abutted by an expanse of gently rolling hills leading up to the base of royal Montana mountains far off in the distance. Tall grass on the hills swayed, almost imperceptibly, in a calm breeze floating across the hills, and the soft echo of the water flowing over rocks in the wide stream that crossed the ranch like a snake uncurling itself. It was the kind of landscape that would inspire painters like Winslow Homer or Georgia O'Keeffe to unroll their blank canvases and take out their brushes.

"I never get tired of this," Savannah mused. "It never gets old."

"For me, either."

There was much that he resented about his father—Jock was harsh, cold at times and unable to admit wrongdoing or express regret—but he'd gotten it right when he'd bought this land. And though maybe Bruce hadn't gotten everything right in his own life, either, he knew, as he admired his wife's profile in the early-evening light, that he *had* gotten it right when he married Savannah.

"I need to go back, I think."

"You okay?"

She nodded, her arms now crossed in front of her body as she turned away from the view. "I suddenly feel so tired. It's been a long day."

"You overdid it." Bruce fell in beside her. "Cooking me dinner."

A shake of her head. "No. That was fun. It's not that. It's that I seem to be going from one appointment to the next to the next now. I can go years without so much as a cold, and yet now, it seems, that's all I'm doing."

Bruce whistled for the dogs playing in the pasture to follow them back to the house.

"Your limp is less noticeable," he told her. "Already."

The bruises on her face had faded to a light yellow and a faint green, a sign of healing, but her speech was still affected, a little slurred and slushy, and as far as he knew, Savannah hadn't had any memories, not even flashes, of the last several years. All of her childhood memories, the memories of her young adulthood, and even the early years of their marriage were still, thankfully, intact. But Savannah still did not have recent memories about the darkest period of their marriage.

"Don't get me wrong—I'm grateful for the help." She ascended the stairs, holding on to the railing, much more slowly than she had descended. "I just wish I didn't *need* the help."

The first time she mustered the nerve to drive herself into town after she was cleared to drive by her neurologist, Savannah decided to meet her friends from work at one of their favorite spots on Main Street.

"How are you?" her friend Maria, a speech-language pathologist at the elementary school where Savannah had worked before the accident, asked after the waitress took their orders.

Savannah took a sip of her soda, enjoying the burn of the carbonation on her throat and the syrupy sweet taste on her tongue. She put her glass down and then said, "Honestly, I don't even know how to answer that."

Deb, a kindergarten teacher whose classroom had been adjacent to Savannah's, put her hand briefly on her arm. "We've all been praying for you."

"Thank you," Savannah said. "I appreciate that. I do. I just want to…feel *normal* again. But I don't even know what normal is anymore."

"I can't imagine," Maria sympathized. "It must be so hard for you."

"It's messy." She frowned in thought. "It's like trying to make sense of a blurry photograph, but no matter how hard I squint, I can't bring my life into focus. I still

can't get my mind around the fact that I've lost *years*."
Savannah shook her head and repeated, *"Years."*

"We're so sorry." Deb's sadness for her was easily
read in her kind, brown eyes.

"It's the little things that really throw me off," she
explained. "Have you ever looked at one of those pictures in the magazine, two side by side pictures, and
you're supposed to figure out what's different about
them?"

Her friends both nodded.

"That's what it's like. But it's not a picture I'm trying to figure out—it's my life. Everyone looks just a
little bit off in my mind, but it takes me some time to
figure out why." Savannah turned to Deb. "Your hair
is past your shoulders now. But for me, it was just a
couple of weeks ago that you were wearing your hair
in a bob and thinking about growing it out. That happens time and time again. Everyone looks just a little
bit off from my memory of them. And sometimes I find
someone staring at me, and I can't be sure if I've met
them before and now they think I'm rude for ignoring
them, or if I have spinach in my teeth."

"You haven't gotten any of your memories back?"
Maria asked.

She shook her head. "But that's not the hardest part.
The hardest part," she continued while her friends lent
her their listening ears, "is my marriage."

Again her friends nodded to signal that they were
listening carefully.

"I know about the divorce, but I don't remember it."
Savannah twisted her wedding band. "Bruce told me,
once when I was still in the hospital, that he still loves

me, but he doesn't touch me. He doesn't kiss me." In a quieter voice she added, "He doesn't sleep in our bed."

"Bruce loves you," Deb interjected. "Everyone knows that. Even when you were getting divorced, we knew that. He just needs some time to switch gears."

"Do you want him to sleep in bed with you?" Maria asked.

Savannah nodded. She really did. Sleeping in their bed, even with the three dogs, felt so lonely. She wanted her husband next to her again.

"Then tell him," Maria encouraged her. "Just tell him."

Her friend's words had rattled around in Savannah's mind all afternoon and late into the evening. The fact that Bruce continued to sleep on the couch was just an accepted fact that neither of them discussed; in fact, they didn't discuss much below the surface. Yes, they were eating dinner together and going for walks. Yes, Bruce had helped her with the garden and taken an interest in her therapy. But they didn't seem to be moving forward together. She resented the divide she felt between them; she resented the figurative wall he had erected as a barrier to keep her at arm's length.

They had already turned in for the night; he went to the couch and she went to the bed. She could hear him snoring lightly from the living room. The more she listened to him sleeping, the more irritated she became with her own silence. Why hadn't she talked to him about the sleeping arrangement? If this second chance at their marriage was going to work, she was going to have to learn how to speak from her heart and tell Bruce what she needed from him. At least, that

was what her therapist had told her in her last session.
And her therapist's observation seemed to align with
Maria's advice.

Savannah carefully pulled her legs out from beneath
the sleeping dogs, trying not to disturb her canine bed-
mates. Barefoot, wearing one of Bruce's white cotton
V-neck undershirts and a pair of bikini underpants,
she petted the dogs, who'd lifted their heads curiously.

"You guys stay here," she whispered. "I've got this
one."

It had been easy for them to put the dogs between
them, focus their attention on them, as another way to
keep them apart. A distraction from the awkward situ-
ation they found themselves in; a distraction from the
strange, wounded state of their marriage. Not this time.

"Bruce."

No response, other than a loud snort and a leg twitch
beneath the blanket.

She reached down and poked his shoulder with her
pointer finger. "Bruce."

That time, her husband's eyes opened wide in surprise, and he sat up, jerking his head back like he was
dodging a punch.

"What the heck, Savannah!" he sputtered. "What's
the matter?"

"Sorry." She tried not to laugh, but failed. "I didn't
mean to scare you."

"I was asleep."

Bruce was always grumbly about being awakened.
She was used to it.

"Are you okay?" He squinted at her. "What's
wrong?"

Savannah sat down on the edge of the couch, forcing her husband to scoot his legs over to make room for her.

"Nothing's wrong," she started, but stopped herself with a shake of her head. "No. That's not true. Something is wrong."

He waited for her to continue, yawning loudly when she paused to collect her thoughts.

"Here's the thing," she restarted. "I don't want you sleeping out here anymore. I want you to sleep in our bed. With me."

Bruce stared at her in the dim light provided by the glow of the three-quarter moon. When he didn't say anything, she asked, "Did you hear me?"

"I heard you." He pushed his body into a more upright position.

That was all he said; she waited for him to continue, yet he didn't.

"I miss having you in bed with me," she added softly. "I miss my husband."

"It's been a long time."

"I know. I know it has been. For you. But for me…"

Bruce blew out his breath, and then he shrugged his shoulders.

"My back's been mighty pissed off about this sleeping arrangement."

Savannah stood up; that was Bruce's way of saying "yes" without saying it directly.

Her husband threw the blanket off his legs and stood up beside her. His body, naked save his boxer briefs, was warm from the blanket. She could feel the heat from his skin; it always felt so good, so secure, to wrap her arms around her husband and feel that warmth of his body transferred to her own skin. It was hard not to reach out to him now; it would be hard to resist reaching out to him when they were in bed together.

"I'm dead tired," Bruce said sleepily, his pillow tucked beneath his arm.

She led the way back to their bed, a bed they had picked out together, a bed they had slept in and made love in and read the Sunday paper together in. There was so much more she wanted from Bruce—kissing and touching and lovemaking and loving words. But this was a start. Getting her husband back to their marital bed was a very good place to start.

Bruce had been dead tired until he climbed into his side of the bed. He found some free real estate for his feet and legs on either side of Buckley's body. He sighed happily as he slid down into the cool, undisturbed sheets on his side of the bed and put his head down on his pillow. He loved this mattress and he'd sorely missed it. And he had a stiff back to prove it.

Savannah was on her side of the bed, Hound Dog's large body sprawled out between them like a chastity belt. She turned on her side, facing away from him, and said good-night. For her, that seemed to be the end of it. She had gotten him back into bed and now she was asleep. But that wasn't the end for him. Now *he* was the one awake. He'd wanted to hold his ground on the couch for his own good—he didn't need to start thinking about making love to Savannah. They'd had an active sex life—that was the one thing that they could always get right. It had taken him a long time to get over the desire to make love to his wife; it had taken him a long time to get used to the idea of having sex with a woman other than Savannah. If this thing blew up in his face, he didn't want to have to detox his body from craving hers.

"Great," he said in a raspy whisper.

"Are you all right?" Savannah asked him, her head turning back a little in his direction.

How should he respond to that? Should he tell her the truth? The scent of her freshly washed hair, the weight of her body on the mattress, the sound of those little sighs she made when she was getting ready to drift off to sleep—all of those things had made his body respond without his permission.

"Go to sleep," he ordered gruffly. "I'm fine."

"Okay," she murmured in a sleepy voice. "'Night."

Bruce usually slept on his back; tonight, he turned on his side, his back to Savannah. He pressed his face into the pillow and tried to ignore the erection in his shorts. How could he be this weak around Savannah? Why did she always seem to have this hold on him, no matter how much he tried to fight it?

He loved her. Still. And he wanted to love her with his body. With his mouth. With his hands. And day by day, dinner by dinner, walk by walk, it was getting harder for him to figure out why he shouldn't make love to his wife. *His* wife.

Savannah wanted the lovemaking—he could feel the tension building between them. A tension that could only be relieved by bringing their bodies together, skin to skin, mouth to mouth.

"Damn," Bruce muttered under his breath as he slipped out of bed.

His body wouldn't give up, and he couldn't go to sleep with a hard-on. This time, Savannah didn't awaken; she just kept right on sleeping while he took a cold shower. Now that he was sleeping in the same bed with his wife, he was gonna have to stop telling his body "no" and start telling it "yes" if he was ever going to get a second of sleep again.

Chapter Five

Savannah had never needed a shrink before she broke a windshield with her head. But now that she had one, she could see how useful they could be.

"Any memories return since the last time we spoke?"

Savannah was lying flat on her back, head on the couch pillow, legs stretched out in front of her. Dr. Rebecca Kind had told her on several occasions that she didn't have to lie down, but she liked talking about her problems in the prone position.

"Not a one."

"Any images, or scents or sounds?"

"Nope." Savannah shook her head. "You know… Kind is a great last name for a shrink." She looked at the counselor. "I bet you hear that a lot."

Dr. Kind, a woman in her late fifties, with salt-and-pepper long, frizzy hair down to her waist, cracked the smallest of smiles. "Let's stay on topic. How are things going in your marriage?"

For this, Savannah felt she needed to sit upright. "So, here's the thing… I did exactly what you suggested—I told Bruce what I needed. And it worked. Sort of."

"How did it work, and what would you like to see improved?"

"Well, it got him back in bed. That's a step in the right direction."

Dr. Kind, her head down, jotted some notes on a pad.

"But…" she continued. "He still won't kiss me or hug me, and God knows there hasn't been even the prospect of sex."

"And you'd like to be physical with your husband."

"Of course. We used to always make love—that never slowed down, even after we'd been married for several years. Now? I've been totally cut off."

"Have you discussed this with Bruce?"

Hands in her lap, Savannah shook her head. "No. He's hard to talk to. He's always been hard to talk to."

"Has communication always been a problem in your marriage?"

She nodded yes. It had always been a problem. And even though she didn't have any memory of it, the fact that they'd resorted to divorce meant that their communication issues had only gotten worse over time.

Dr. Kind put her pen down on top of the pad of paper and then rested one hand on top of the other. "Have you spoken to Bruce at all about what caused the divorce?"

"No. I'm not ready for that. *We're* not ready for that."

"What frightens you the most about finding out what your mind won't remember?"

Savannah knew what frightened her the most, but it was hard for her to put her thoughts into words, even in this private, safe environment. If she found out what broke their marriage apart while they were so disconnected, then her marriage to Bruce would surely fail for a second time. And no matter what had happened during the last several years—whoever *that* Savannah was—this Savannah was deeply in love with her husband, and she did not want to risk losing him again.

"I have a suggestion." Dr. Kind filled in the silence. "I'd like for Bruce to join us next time."

Savannah's eyebrows popped upward. Bruce didn't mind her going to a shrink, but he didn't believe in paying good money to spill your guts to strangers when you could just walk out to any pasture and tell your problems to a cow for free.

"I don't think he'll come."

"Don't assume. Give him the chance to say yes or no." Dr. Kind looked at her wristwatch and then checked the clock on the wall. "Good. Let's end here today."

"What's on your agenda for today?" Bruce asked his wife after he took a sip of coffee.

Savannah wasn't used to having so much free time during the summer—she always volunteered to teach during summer at her elementary school—so it didn't surprise him that she had been keeping herself occupied by cooking almost every meal for him. They had opted to skip the big family Sunday breakfast; even though he'd had a heart-to-heart with his brothers about Savannah, some of them just couldn't treat his wife like they had before. It made Savannah uncomfortable, and he didn't want to force her to spend concentrated time with his family right now. After his brothers saw that their marriage was going to last—if it did—then things would work out eventually. That was his rationale.

"I was thinking about spending some time with Mom and Dad," she replied distractedly. "What's on yours?"

Bruce leaned his forearms on the table, his eyes drinking in the sight of the simple pleasure of having his wife sitting across from him again. "It's Sunday."

"Uh-huh."

"How 'bout we get back to our Sunday tradition?"

Savannah, who had been answering emails and texts on her phone, finally looked up at him. When she smiled at him, a smile that reached those pretty eyes of hers, it sent a pang into the pit of his stomach. This woman still had the power to wreck him with her smile; he loved to be the one to inspire that smile, and he lived for the moments when he could make her laugh.

"What do you have in mind?"

"Anything you want."

Her smile broadened, and that pang in his stomach grew stronger. He had spent most of his days during their marriage thinking of ways to make Savannah happy—that was his mission, because she had the same mission for him. Maybe it was time for him to risk a little to get a bigger return. Much like her garden, Savannah had been wilting right in front of him. And he had a feeling, a very strong feeling, that he was a big part of it.

"Drinking Horse Mountain," Savannah decided. "Something new."

A cloud entered her eyes when she asked a second later, "It is new, right?"

"Yes," he reassured her. "It's new."

They filled a backpack with water and food, supplies for the dogs, and Savannah called her mom to let her know that she would be spending the day with Bruce.

"Mom wants to know if we want to come over after for an early dinner." His wife held her phone against her body to muffle the sound of his answer.

It was easy for him to read the anticipation on Savannah's face—she loved her family, she loved him—and it would be the perfect capstone on her day if she could see her folks. So he agreed. After hiking, in-laws.

They loaded the dogs into the backseat of his truck, and he held the passenger door open for Savannah and helped her climb into the passenger seat. She had made some progress in physical therapy, but even though the limp was barely noticeable, her leg was still weak.

"Windows up or windows down?" Savannah asked happily when he climbed behind the wheel.

"Down."

"That's what I thought, too."

Bruce lowered the windows halfway in the back seat so the dogs could stick their heads out, as they liked to do, without risking that they would jump out. He cranked the engine, but before he shifted into Drive, he asked, "What are you in the mood for?"

As with everything, his wife put her due consideration into the question of music choice. After a minute of thought, she said with a question in her tone, "Motown."

Bruce scrolled through his phone with a nod. "Motown it is."

On their way off the ranch, they saw Noah riding in one of the pastures. He waved to his younger brother but didn't stop. He did stop when he saw Jock and Lilly rocking on the front porch of the main house.

"Why the hell weren't you two at breakfast?" Jock hobbled down the steps. He wasn't all that old, but his spine didn't seem to know that. His father had a couple of herniated discs in his back that he refused to have fixed. So the rancher and patriarch walked in a side to side motion, often with his hand on his back.

"It's my fault, Dad." Savannah was quick to take the blame. "I was too tired for a big family breakfast."

"Bah." Jock rested his hands on the open truck window. "Where're you off to now?"

Savannah looked at him with an excited smile before she answered Jock. "Bruce is taking me hiking up at Drinking Horse Mountain."

The rancher gave a slight nod, and pushed away from the truck. "Have a good time, then."

Bruce couldn't remember the last time he drove away from the ranch on a Sunday, with his wife next to him, his hiking gear packed, and his dogs ready for an adventure. The day was as beautiful as a day could get, with a clear, cloudless, turquoise-blue sky, and a coolness in the air that made it feel more like fall than summer. Bruce cranked up the tunes, with his right hand on the steering wheel, and let his left arm rest on the open window. The sun would warm the skin on his arm, and then the breeze would cool it of, and his wife was sitting next to him, singing off-key and loudly, as she always did, to Stevie Wonder's "Signed, Sealed Delivered, I'm Yours…"

They didn't speak much on the way to the recreational park—not in an awkward "I don't have anything to say to you" kind of way. It was comfortable. Like it used to be for them. From Sugar Creek Ranch, they drove through downtown Bozeman and then State Route 86 to the figure-eight shaped hiking trail. It was one of the few trails they hadn't visited; they loved to set out together with the dogs and hike the abundant trails in Montana. After their marriage fell apart, Bruce hadn't had the desire to hike alone or with friends. It had been "their" thing, and without Savannah, hiking lost its appeal.

"It's crowded." Savannah had turned down the music as they approached the park. "Oh! There's a spot right there."

"Got it." Bruce pulled into one of the few free spaces just before another truck got there.

He shut off the engine. "Are you sure you're up for this?"

Ever since the accident, she had developed a mild case of social anxiety, and he wasn't sure how she'd feel about sharing the trail with large groups of hikers.

"I'll be okay," she told him, but she had a worried look in her eyes as she took a survey of her surroundings.

Bruce made sure he was at her door to help her down to the ground before he unloaded the dogs and slung the backpack onto his back. Savannah used her standard walking stick, a stick that had pins from most of the trails she had tackled since she was a teenager, as well as holding Hound Dog's leash.

"They have two trail types—we'll take the easy route this time." He shortened his stride to keep pace with Savannah.

She nodded in response because she was too busy admiring the beautiful landscape that encompassed the forty-acre park. "This is incredible. Isn't it?"

"It sure is." They had always agreed on the beauty of Montana. They were both natives, and they both couldn't imagine any other place in the world to call home.

Mindful of Savannah's healing concussion and her leg weakness, Bruce was careful to hold their pace to a slower one than was typical for them. Every time Savannah would speed up, excited to see more of the landscape unfolding before them, he would be the one to remind her to slow down. He got them to take frequent water breaks, and pointed out benches to rest more often than he needed. Her health, her recovery, mattered to him. He couldn't seem to get the image of her lying in the hospital bed, hooked up to every beeping machine in the room, her face swollen, in a coma, out of his head. That was an image that wouldn't wash, no matter how much he tried to scrub it from his mind.

"Let's sit down over there." Bruce pointed to the next bench on the trail.

"Again?" Savannah's cheeks were flushed red, and she had beads of sweat rolling down her neck.

"Why not?" he asked her. "You got somewhere else to be?"

She frowned at him. "No."

He dug a bottle of water out of the backpack and

handed it to her. While his wife cooled off, Bruce took the three dogs down to Bridger Creek so they could hydrate and cool off, as well. Savannah laughed loudly and freely when the dogs, now sopping wet from the creek, descended upon her and shook themselves dry. She was sprayed from three directions and was splattered from her waist to her face by water from their fur.

"You cooled off now?" Bruce joined her on the bench.

Savannah was picking some dog hair off her tongue. "Yeah. I think so."

They sat together, silent, the three dogs at their feet, taking in the brown-and-green mountain landscape before them.

"This is heaven on earth." Savannah sighed.

Bruce looked at her, enjoying the view of his wife as much as the scenery provided by Drinking Horse.

"You know what this reminds me of?" he asked her, gesturing to the mountains.

"What?"

"All those movies they used to show us in school when we were kids about the outdoors."

They decided to eat a snack before continuing on their hike. Savannah finished her last bite of her protein bar, balled up the wrapper and put it in the front pocket of the backpack.

"I couldn't believe that Liam and Cynthia got divorced," his wife said to him. "When did that happen?"

Bruce put his empty wrapper in the front pocket as well, then zipped it shut. "It's been at least a year now."

Savannah shook her head in disbelief. "What happened?"

"I'm not too sure." He flicked a bug off his arm. "Liam doesn't like to talk about it, so I don't push him."

"Does he get to see the kids?"

Bruce stood up and hoisted the backpack onto his back before offering his hand to his wife. "He'll be getting them for a month this summer. But that's about all I know."

He was glad when Savannah dropped the subject—the more they talked about Liam's divorce, the more it made him think about their near miss. They walked the entire trail together, little by little, taking it slow, taking their time. He took pictures of Savannah on the trail for her to text to her family and friends, and a fellow hiker had offered to take a picture of them, as a couple, with the dogs, on the Kevin Mundy Memorial Bridge.

"Send that to me," Bruce said to her after they both looked at the first picture that had been taken of them since her return to the ranch.

By the time they got home, they had spent an entire Sunday together as a couple, and it felt more like old times to Bruce than it had in a long while. They had tired themselves out on the hike, built up a heck of an appetite, and then they'd cooked out at Savannah's parents' house, with Savannah's sister Justine and her fiancé, Mike. The fact that he was back at his in-laws' house, a home he'd loved and in which he had always felt welcome, was like a dream in motion. He'd thought it had all been lost.

"I don't know about you, but I am tired and stuffed." Savannah laughed tiredly.

Bruce shut the front door behind them, hung his hat on the hook and dropped the backpack next to the door.

"I'm right there with you."

Instead of going straight into the bedroom, Savannah turned on the lamp next to the couch and then circled back to him. She surprised him by wrapping her arms around his waist and giving him a quick hug.

"Thank you for today." Savannah dropped her arms, her face upturned.

It would have been so natural to kiss those lips—lips that were small and peach-colored, and always felt so soft beneath his own. She wanted him to kiss her—he knew that look in her eyes—but he just couldn't bring himself to do it.

"You're welcome," he told her as she turned away from him.

"Do you mind if I take a shower first?"

"No. You go on ahead. I'll go after you."

He sat down on the couch, Buckley next to him and Murphy at his feet, in the silence. He didn't feel like turning on the TV or listening to music; he just wanted to sit there and get his mind right. God, how he wanted to trust in his marriage. He wanted to make love to Savannah without any fear that she was going to leave him one day. She'd already ripped out his guts once—how could he give her the chance to do it again?

"Bruce!"

"Yeah?"

"Could you get me a towel out of the dryer?" Savannah called to him from the master bathroom. "I forgot to get one out!"

"Okay!"

Bruce went into the mudroom, opened the dryer and pulled out the towels Savannah had put in to dry before they left. For a split second, he was taken back in time, to another day when he had pulled towels out of the dryer—a day he had tried so hard to forget. He shook off the memory and carried the towels into the bedroom, dropped the pile onto the bed, and grabbed one for his wife.

They had designed the master bathroom shower together—both favoring a roomy shower built for two, with two showering stations at either end of the stall. Two sides of the shower were made completely of glass. Bruce had made it a point not to go into the bathroom when Savannah was showering, because there was no way *not* to see her naked.

"I'll just leave it on the counter."

"Oh, no. I'm so cold. Just hand it to me, would you? Please?"

Savannah was his wife. He had seen her naked thousands of times—and he had enjoyed every moment. In his eyes, she was a lithe, nymph-like beauty, and he loved seeing her body unclothed. Why was he trying so hard to avoid it now? Because he'd have to deal with the hard-on it would surely arouse?

Instead of averting his eyes or trying to avoid Savannah's nakedness any longer, Bruce walked straight over to the shower with the towel.

Savannah had the door of the shower cracked open, and the water was off.

"Thank you." She smiled at him as she hugged the towel to her body. Her right breast was round and full, with droplets of water clinging to the puckered nipple. In moments past, he would have bent down to lick the water from her nipple; he would have taken her, still damp from the shower, to the bed and made love to her.

Savannah caught him staring at her breast, and she didn't cover her body. Instead, she met his gaze when he brought his eyes to hers, and there was an invitation there for him to see.

As much as he wanted to love her—as much as his body wanted to love her—he just couldn't seem to take that leap of faith.

The moment was lost; Savannah wrapped the towel around her body and stepped out of the shower. While he took his shower, she closed up the house, took care of the dogs for the night, and was in bed by the time he emerged from the bathroom.

It had become a pattern for the dogs to create a barrier between the two sides of the bed, his and Savannah's. Bruce turned off the light and lay flat on his back, listening to the sound of Hound Dog licking his private parts.

"Really, Hound Dog?" he complained, "Is that necessary?"

Savannah laughed. "I find it to be oddly soothing."

Bruce turned his head to look at his wife. "Good night, Savannah."

"Good night."

Not right away, but before he drifted off to sleep, Savannah added, "Dr. Kind thinks it would be a good idea if you come to my next appointment."

Bruce didn't respond; he listened.

"Will you think about it?"

When he didn't answer right away, she said, "Bruce? Will you?"

"Yes," he said before he closed his eyes again. "I'll think about it."

Chapter Six

He had gone with her to speech therapy and to physical therapy—he had gone with her to her neurologist, to her internist, and he had dropped her off at her psychologist. But he hadn't imagined that he would be involved in her meetings with the psychologist. Perhaps that was naive thinking on his part.

"Thank you for coming today, Mr. Brand."

"Bruce," he corrected. "You're welcome."

Dr. Kind was wearing a long, flowy skirt with sandals, and her toenails were painted a very deep shade of purple. She folded her hands on top of an open notepad, drawing his eyes back to her face.

Savannah was sitting on one end of the three-seater couch, while he was at the other end. Bruce wondered if Dr. Kind had already made a note on her pad about that.

"Is there anything you'd like to say to start, Savannah?"

Savannah quickly glanced his way; her shoulders were stiff, and she was biting the inside of her cheek, which was a sure sign that she was a bundle of nerves on the inside.

"Um, sure." His wife cleared her throat. "I just feel stuck." She turned her head so she could look him in the eye. "I think that we're stuck. And I want to move forward. I want us to be like we were before."

It took Bruce a second to process what Savannah had said. He thought that he was here for her—to help her with her feelings relating to the memory loss. He wasn't here for marriage counseling. He told Dr. Kind as much.

"Savannah has done a substantial amount of inner work related to her individual concerns. Inevitably, we have to deal with problems related to the marriage."

Dr. Kind continued. "How do you feel the marriage is working?"

Maybe it was the soothing tone of Dr. Kind's voice or the scent of lavender in the air, but one minute he was clammed up and the next he was spilling his guts to a woman he'd just met. Dr. Kind scribbled furiously as he spoke, and when he managed to get himself to shut up, she looked up from her notes.

"Thank you for sharing that, Bruce," the psychologist said. "Let me see if I can recast what I've heard you say. While you understand that, for Savannah, the fighting and the separation and everything leading up to the divorce is not a part of her current memory, for you, every fight, every attorney meeting, every attorney *bill* is very real, and still very raw. Yes?"

Bruce nodded.

"Do you hear that, Savannah?"

Savannah, who hadn't stopped chewing on the side of her cheek yet, gave a little nod.

"What I hear in all that you've shared with me today, Bruce, is that you are afraid to invest in this marriage because you are concerned that Savannah can leave the marriage again."

"I don't know why I left," Savannah interjected; she reached out across the divide and touched his arm. "But I'm not leaving again."

"Do you hear that, Bruce?"

"I hear it," he acknowledged. "But what happens when your memory comes back?" He said this directly to his wife before addressing the therapist. "I personally think that we need to talk about the elephant in the room, about what caused the divorce in the first place. That way we don't have to spend all of this time working on our marriage if all she's going to want is to go through with the divorce."

"Are you ready for that, Savannah?"

He hated the fact that he was the cause of the color draining from Savannah's face.

"No."

Dr. Kind checked her watch. "Okay. We have a couple of minutes left. Bruce, Savannah has made a promise to you that she isn't going to proceed with the divorce. If you want your marriage to work, you're going to have to let go of the pain of these last several years and try to move forward. And, Savannah, you need to be patient with Bruce."

The therapist closed her pad and put it on the table next to her chair. She leaned forward, hands clasped, her forearms resting on her thighs. "Savannah, I want you to sit next to Bruce. Bruce, turn to your wife and take her hands."

Like a robot, he followed her direction. This woman had a way of getting him to do things that he wouldn't normally do on demand.

"Tell Bruce what you need."

Savannah took a steadying breath. "I need you to stop calling me 'Savannah.' You only used to do that when you were mad at me. I need you to hold my hand, and sit with me on the couch and…I need you to kiss me 'hello' and 'goodbye.'"

"Bruce?" Dr. Kind prompted. "What do you need from Savannah?"

He couldn't believe he was in this moment; he hadn't anticipated it. Savannah, her hands in his, her eyes focused so intently on his face, was listening to him in a way that perhaps she never had before.

"Tell me," Savannah said softly.

"Don't ever—" Bruce stared into his wife's eyes "—say that you want a divorce."

"I won't." She whispered the interjection.

"Ever again."

Savannah felt emotionally drained after the session with Dr. Kind. She had imagined that the therapist wouldn't be able to get more than two words out of her husband, but as it turned out, Bruce had a lot bottled inside that he needed to get off his chest. Savannah imagined that no one was more surprised than Bruce himself. He had been quiet on the ride home; when they arrived back at the ranch, he went out to his workshop and she went to her garden.

Dr. Kind had left them with homework to do with a request that they both return the following week. The homework was for them to start dating. Even though they were married, they needed to treat this as a new, fragile relationship and nurture it as such.

"Look up," Jessie instructed, holding an eyeliner in her hand.

Savannah looked up to the bathroom ceiling, trying not to blink as her sister-in-law brought a pointy pencil close to her left eye.

"But I never wear eyeliner," she told Bruce's sister. "A little mascara, a little lip gloss and I'm good to go."

"Keep looking up," Jessie said. "This is Naughty Nutmeg, and it will make your hazel eyes pop right out of your face."

Savannah pulled away and blinked her eyes several times. "Do I want them to pop out of my face? Has fashion really changed that much in three years?"

"Don't wipe them or you'll smear it, and we'll have to start all over!" her sister-in-law exclaimed.

Still blinking, Savannah smiled at her. "That was a little amnesia humor for you."

Jessie screwed up her face. "I got it. Let me look at your eyes."

After a moment, her sister-in-law gave her a smile and a nod of approval before stepping aside so Savannah could see the finished product.

"Well?" Jessie asked impatiently after a moment of silence.

Savannah studied her reflection in the mirror. For her *second* first date with Bruce Brand, she had gone to have her hair dyed a deep mahogany brown; this color was much closer to the color she last remembered. She was growing out those awful bangs—she couldn't imagine what she was thinking with that hair travesty—but at least it could be fixed with time. Jessie had gone shopping with her and "styled" her; her sister-in-law actually convinced her to buy a midnight-blue wrap dress and strappy heels. Jessie had also taken her to the makeup counter to buy new cosmetics.

"I think you made me actually look glamorous."

"That's what I was going for," Jessie said proudly.

Savannah stood up and hugged her sister-in-law. Afterward, she brushed Jessie's long, pin-straight, black hair over her shoulders.

"You're so grown up," she said wistfully. "And so *tall*!"

She couldn't stop herself from remembering Jessie as a gawky, awkward fifteen-year-old who was worried about acne and her breasts not coming in fast enough. Now, she was eighteen, a willowy beauty who had recently graduated from high school and had absolutely nothing to worry about in the décolletage area.

Jessie hugged her again. "I'm glad you're back. I missed you."

"Do you think your brother is going to think I've lost my mind getting this dressed up?"

Her sister-in-law uncapped the new lip gloss on the counter, applied it to her full lips and smacked them together. "Please. He's gonna love the fact that you put in so much effort. What do you think of this color on me?"

"Lovely."

"That's what I thought." Jessie pouted her lips and posed in the mirror, then took out her phone and leaned her head next to Savannah's. "Here. Snapchat."

After the photo op, Savannah took one last look at herself in the full-length mirror on the back of the bathroom door. She pulled at the belt on her dress, then fidgeted with her bra straps. Jessie had managed to cover the puckered red scar on her forehead, and with her hair changed back to nearly its original color, if she squinted, she looked more like the woman she remembered from several years back than the one she awakened to in the hospital.

"Well." She tilted her head. "I hope Bruce loves me in this."

Those were the words that she said for Jessie to hear, but in her mind, she thought—

I hope my husband falls in love with me again in this.

The thirty minutes of waiting for Bruce to pick her up was nerve-racking for Savannah. They consisted of sweating, pacing, sitting back down on the couch, checking her phone, sending texts to her sisters, video-chatting with her sisters and finally landing back in the bathroom to "just in case" urinate and use the hair dryer to dry off the sweat stains under her arms. They had agreed to make this as much like a real first date as possible, so Bruce was getting ready in the main house, while she was to wait for him at their home.

Pacing in the living room, talking to Hound Dog, who was watching her curiously, Savannah wished that she hadn't insisted on getting ready so early. She didn't want to be late for her second first date with Bruce, but by the time the man arrived, she would have sweated through half her makeup.

"Oh, thank goodness," Savannah said to Hound Dog.

She walked over to the window to peek out; Bruce had just pulled up and was about to get out.

"Aw," she told her canine companion. "He washed the truck."

Savannah scurried back to the couch, sat down on the edge of the cushion, smoothed her skirt over her knees and cupped her hands together and rested them on her thighs.

Unexpectedly, instead of just opening the front door of his own house, Bruce knocked. Hound Dog went to the door, his tail wagging. Savannah moved out of her perfectly staged pose on the couch and opened the door for her husband.

"Hello." Bruce was standing in the doorway holding long-stemmed red roses.

"Hi." Savannah accepted the flowers, brought the fat, bright red flowers up to her nose and inhaled the sweetness.

She met her husband's gaze over the top of the flowers; now that she saw him, she was glad she had gone all out for this date. He was wearing a new pair of dark wash denim jeans, his dress cowboy boots and a new button-down shirt, in her favorite color, forest green. If she had a tail, just like Hound Dog, she'd be wagging it for Bruce too.

"I'll just put these in some water."

Bruce followed her to the kitchen; while she cut the ends of the flowers, Bruce located a vase in a cabinet above the refrigerator.

"Thank you." Savannah admired the flowers, now in the vase. "They're beautiful."

As Bruce stood closer to her than usual, the scent of his woodsy cologne, her favorite, mingled with the strong, sweet smell of the roses in the most tantalizing way.

"You look beautiful."

His compliment, so simple, so quietly delivered, brought her to tears, which she quickly pushed back; in every way he could say, without words, Bruce was telling her that he was going to try to make their marriage work. That he was willing to give her—their—life together an honest chance.

"You look handsome." She brushed a piece of lint from his arm.

"Shall we?" Her husband offered her that same arm.

Happily, Savannah tucked her hand into the crook of Bruce's arm. "Where are we going?"

"It's a surprise," he told her. "Is that okay?"

She laughed—for no reason at all other than she felt happy. "Sure. I'm actually starting to kind of like them."

Bruce didn't realize until he shut the passenger-side door to the truck that his palms were sweating. From the time he'd pulled up to his cabin, to the moment he had his wife securely in the truck, he had felt slightly sick to his stomach. He was nervous—nervous as all get-out, actually—to take his wife out on a date.

"The truck looks nice," Savannah said to him. She had always nagged him about using the floorboard on the passenger side of his truck as a trash can of sorts; he'd wanted to make sure that he cleaned the inside and the outside of the truck for their date.

"Any requests?"

"No," Savannah said faintly. "Surprise me."

After Bruce dropped Hound Dog off with Lilly and

Jock, who were already watching Buckley and Murphy, he chose a CD and lowered the volume so it was more like background music.

"Ah," She dropped her head back on the headrest and smiled. "I love Patsy Cline."

"I remember." He remembered everything about his wife—all of those little things that made her his wife. In particular, he remembered the fragrance she was wearing tonight; with some floral and white musk notes, that scent evoked so many memories of Savannah. Always Savannah.

They drove toward Bozeman. As the sun was setting on the horizon in the rearview mirror, the inside of the truck cab was washed with a gold-and-blue romantic light. This was where he always wanted to be—with this woman, by her side, sharing the small pleasures of life and tackling the tough challenges together. Somewhere along the way, things had gone so terribly wrong between them. And yet, here she was, back in his life. It felt like he was being blessed by God, but he couldn't figure out why.

"This is the best night I can remember," Savannah told him softly.

"It hasn't even begun yet." He glanced at her pretty profile.

"Yes, it has." She touched his arm briefly. "And it's perfect."

When Bruce pulled into a parking space in front of the South 9th Bistro, a restaurant that held a lot of meaning for them as a couple, all of the pieces fell into place for Savannah; Bruce was re-creating their first date, from the long-stemmed roses, to Patsy Cline, to the restaurant.

"Bruce…" Savannah unhooked her seat belt. "You're such a romantic."

"I try to be." He took the keys out of the ignition. "For you."

He had reserved their table on the second floor of the quaint restaurant with big-city cuisine. As always, Bruce held the chair for her, making sure she was settled before he seated himself.

"Are you up for a bottle of wine?" he asked her.

In the candlelight of the private table, Savannah couldn't stop herself from speaking her thoughts. "I have always loved sitting across from you at a table. You are so handsome."

That brought out his half smile, a half smile that she had fallen in love with very early on in their courtship.

"And yes—to the wine."

He ordered her favorite merlot, and with every passing moment she felt more spoiled than the next. Although she had believed in the impact of their session with Dr. Kind, the extent to which the session had blown through the barrier that had been holding them back was beyond her wildest expectation. Bruce seemed to be "all-in," and she knew this Bruce—once he locked in on what he wanted, he never gave up.

"Are you hungry?"

Savannah laughed. "You are going to have to roll me out of here, sir. Because I am starving, and I am going to eat like a famine is imminent."

Over their favorite appetizer, escargots, they talked about nothing—and in a way, they talked about everything. They talked about the ranch, and their families and how she missed her job. They talked about her desire to put a greenhouse in the backyard and his desire to add a deck to their cabin. It was a lovely moment and she cherished it.

After the waiter cleared their appetizer plates and refilled their wineglasses, Bruce smiled at her in a way that she hadn't seen since before that awful day she awakened in the hospital.

"Do you remember when we met?" He leaned forward, his eyes locked with hers.

"Of course." She leaned in to the table, as well. "First grade, Mrs. Coleman's class. As I recall, you heckled me during show-and-tell..."

"That's a lie."

"I brought my painted lady caterpillar aquarium, and you heckled me."

"I don't remember it that way at all."

She crossed her arms in front of her chest in feigned anger. "Even back then you were the most popular kid in the class. And I was..."

"The smartest kid in the class," he filled in.

"And the nerdiest."

She'd had buck teeth, pigtails, glasses—the works. And, she had been a precocious reader and had begun to read the dictionary when most kids her age were still tackling Clifford books.

"I picked on you because I thought you were cute," Bruce added.

"You should be ashamed of yourself, Brand," she teased him. "You tortured me for years."

"Thank God you have a forgiving nature."

Savannah uncrossed her arms, leaned toward him

and lowered her voice for his ears only. "I thank God for *your* forgiving nature."

Before the tone of the dinner could switch from up-beat to serious, the main course arrived—Bruce had ordered his standard favorite black truffle New York strip steak, bloody in the center. And she couldn't say no to the filet, medium well, with the most delicious cognac-peppercorn sauce. They both took their time, savored the food, savored the company—savored the moment.

"Here's to you." Savannah held out her glass after she had cleaned her plate.

Bruce wiped his mouth, dropped his napkin on his empty plate and raised his glass.

"To us." He touched his glass to hers.

"To us," she agreed.

The waiter swung by their table to clear their plates; he asked the inevitable question, "Did you leave room for dessert?"

Savannah and Bruce locked eyes.

"Are you up for it, Brand?" He issued the challenge.

"Are you?"

Bruce gave a little laugh at her bravado—he knew her eyes were always bigger than her stomach.

"One Black Beast," her husband told the waiter. "Two forks."

Chapter Seven

Bruce held the door for Savannah; she was laughing as they walked out into the crisp night air, and his heart fed on that sound.

"You just had to go for the Black Beast, didn't you?" She bumped into him playfully.

Chocolate torte, dark chocolate ganache, blood orange chocolate mousse and more whipped cream than should be legal, the Black Beast was the dessert that they couldn't resist on their first date, but had wished they had.

"I feel like I need to walk off the Beast and the wine." He admired the way the light breeze was blowing wisps of hair around her face.

Not thinking twice, he moved a wayward strand of hair away from her mouth. His thumb lingered for the briefest of moments on her lower lip.

"Can you walk in those heels?" he asked.

"I think I can hold my own. As long as you let me hold on to your arm every now and then."

An evening after-dinner walk was a part of his plan for this second first date. He'd wanted to show Savannah, without having to say the words, that he wanted to start doing his part to repair their marriage. No, it wasn't going to happen overnight for him. But if he wasn't going to make an effort, put some trust in his wife, risk his heart a bit, then he should let Savannah go right now. *That* he wasn't willing to do.

Bruce wasn't under any illusion that every day would be like this; there were plenty of rough waters ahead. Yet, as he walked down the street with his wife's hand tucked into the crook of his arm, he felt like a king among men. He was proud of his wife—who she was as a person, her values, her choice to pursue her passion of educating children over the amount of money she could make. Her outward prettiness was quirky more than classical—it was the beauty he saw on her inside, once he was mature enough himself to notice it, that made him fall hard for the brainiest, biggest bookworm in Bozeman, Montana.

"Do you remember the first time I kissed you?" On a darkened street lined with mature trees, Bruce asked his wife a question for the second time that evening.

Suddenly, Savannah inhaled when she realized where he had taken her.

"Story Mansion." Her fingers tightened on his arm. "You kissed me first, and then asked me out. Totally backward."

They had both attended Montana State University directly after high school; he had continued with sports and joined a fraternity. Savannah had focused, as she always did, on academic and civic-minded activities. He became the president of his fraternity, Sigma Phi Epsilon, which happened to own and occupy one of the oldest landmarks in Bozeman: Story Mansion.

They both stopped, mesmerized by the historic house built in 1910; it was one of the few remaining three-block mansions in Montana, and for over a decade, the house had been preserved as a public state historical treasure and park after being purchased by the city of Bozeman. Eighty years before the city bought the mansion and saved it from development, his fraternity, SAE, had owned it.

"This brings back a lot of really good memories," Bruce mused. His days living in the Story Mansion, partying with his frat brothers, drinking too much and chasing coeds when he was "off-again" with Kerri were some of the best in his life.

On the other hand, as a volunteer member of the Bozeman Historical Society, Savannah had vehemently opposed the use of an irreplaceable cornerstone of Montana's rich history as a house of depravity for a bunch of oversexed frat boys.

"Uh-huh."

His wife remained unimpressed by his past history with this house that she loved.

"Don't forget," he teased her. "SAE was considered a good steward of this place for over eighty years."

Savannah let that comment slip away into the night without a response.

"Come on." Bruce grabbed her hand and began to lead her down the shadowed path to the front steps of the mansion.

"Wait." This was said in a loud whisper. "It's *closed*."

"We're not going inside."

Bruce led her up the front steps of the mansion, while she continued to protest in harsh whispers. Savannah stopped at yellow lights, never walked on grass if there was a Keep Off sign, while he liked to break a rule every once in a while.

On the porch now, he put his arm around his wife's shoulders, holding her next to him, as they looked out at the view of the street where they were just standing.

"We are *trespassing*."

"This is a public park."

"That's currently *closed*."

"Just stand here with me, sugar." Bruce leaned his head down to hers. "Just for a minute."

His wife stopped protesting and stood very still beside him, as if she wanted to turn into an unnoticeable statue in case a passerby spotted them.

"*This* is where we first kissed," Bruce reminded her. "Right here."

Yes, he had gone to school with Savannah all of his life; but he'd never really known her, other than the immature labels he had assigned her in his young mind: nerd, brain, Goody Two-shoes. But the day that a passionate, self-possessed Savannah lit into him about the impact of his fraternity's debauchery on Story Mansion during a pledge keg party, *that* was the day that they truly met. She had verbally sliced and diced him in a way no one in his life had ever done, and instead of being offended, he'd felt attracted to her fiery, intelligent eyes, her command of the English language, her flushed cheeks and the little gap between her two front teeth.

She didn't care that he was the president of the fraternity, or heir to Sugar Creek Ranch or the captain of the football team. Savannah cared about deeper issues, and he found himself oddly hooked from that day forward. He'd taken her tongue-lashing, found her devotion to an old, kind of smelly house rather charming, and the passion he saw in her hazel eyes sexy. Just as she was wrapping up her ardent plea for Story Mansion, Bruce had kissed Savannah. Right then, right there, without any warning. It had, quite honestly, been a shock to them both. And that unexpected kiss had been the start of their love affair.

"I admit I was a little too zealous back then," she whispered back. "But I just believed so deeply that this beautiful place needed to be preserved for generations to come. This is our history—history that we can see and feel and imagine what life could have been like for the people who came before."

Bruce turned her in his arms as he murmured, "There it is."

In the soft yellow light from the street, he read the question on her face, which he answered.

"That passion I fell in love with." He brushed her hair back away from her shoulders. "Right here on this porch."

This was the place that he wanted to solidify his recommitment to their marriage; this was the spot where he wanted to cross the invisible line he had between himself and Savannah.

Bruce cupped her face with his hands and touched his lips to hers; just that simple light touch wasn't enough. Her lips parted and her arms slipped around his body. His wife, his lovely wife, made a pleasurable little sound as he deepened the kiss. They stood together, holding each other, kissing as if for the first time, surrounded by the brick and stone and wood that had withstood the test of time for over one hundred years.

"I love you." Savannah had her head resting on his chest, her arms around him holding him so tightly.

Bruce closed his eyes for a second, pushing back a rush of emotion. He thought he'd never kiss Savannah again; to have her back in his life, even after all this time passed, still seemed like a dream from which he did not want to awaken.

"And I love you, my beautiful wife." He kissed the top of her head. "I love you."

Bruce sent a text to his stepmother to ask her to keep the dogs overnight. Tonight, Savannah realized, was the night that her husband wanted to be all about them as a couple. Everything he had planned for her, from the roses, to the dinner, to the evening walk and stolen kisses on the porch of Story Mansion—he had pulled out all of the romantic stops. He was wooing her and it had worked. All of the distance she had wanted to put between them, in reaction to the emotional walls he had erected, fell away.

Still a little bit tipsy, Savannah twirled in the living room when they arrived home, making her skirt swing out around her legs. Dizzy, she laughed and fell back onto the couch.

"This was the most amazing night." She smiled at her handsome husband. "Thank you."

Bruce hung his hat on the hook just inside the door; there was a look in his stunning blue eyes that touched her in the most intimate places in her body.

"Is the night over?" he asked her.

Savannah's laugh quieted. "I don't want it to be."

Bruce crossed to her, offered her his hand.

She slipped her hand into her husband's warm, calloused one. He helped her stand and then led her into the bedroom. Tonight, there wouldn't be a canine wall separating them. Tonight, there wouldn't be anything between them.

Savannah sat on the edge of the bed, leaned down to unbuckle the straps on her heels and slipped her feet out of the shoes while Bruce lit candles in the bathroom. The physical side of their marriage had never waned, at least not in her memory; the lovemaking had been just as passionate, and satisfying and adventurous as it had been from the first time they loved each other. The moment she heard her husband running the water in the oversized claw-foot tub, specifically selected because it was roomy enough for two, Savannah knew what Bruce had in mind. Yes, they enjoyed making love in the bed. But making love in the tub, with the slippery, warm water as a natural lubricant, had always been their favorite spot.

She joined her husband in the bathroom; Savannah unbuttoned his shirt, exposing his chest. She ran her hands over his chest, lightly scratching the chest hair and skin with her fingernails. He stood still for her, letting her explore his body, letting her kiss his neck before she slipped his shirt off his shoulders and tossed it on the bathroom counter.

"Hmm." She ran her hand over the bulge in his jeans.

Bruce was ready for her; and without him so much as touching her with his lips or his fingers, her body was ready for him.

Her husband hooked his finger on the belt of her wrap dress and tugged her forward; he kissed her, deep, long—a promise of the pleasure to come. Bruce undressed her then, unwrapping the layers of her dress and undergarments until she was naked before him. No man had ever made her feel as beautiful or desirable as Bruce did. He loved her from the inside outward.

She closed her eyes with a little gasp when he kissed her neck while his fingers stroked the sensitive skin of her breasts and her stomach and the curve of her derriere. Savannah reached between their bodies to unbutton and unzip his jeans.

"You're shivering," Bruce said as he kissed the side of her neck. "Get in the tub and I'll be right behind you."

Savannah sank down into the hot water, sighing at the feel of the water enveloping her body. She turned off the water, not wanting it to spill over the edge of the tub when her husband joined her.

"It's perfect in here." She arched her back to submerge her hair in the water.

Bruce watched her as he stripped off his jeans. Until she'd met her husband, she had never known how much she enjoyed having a man watch her, to admire her naked body. She had discovered her own true sexuality with Bruce.

In the candlelight, her husband's body, to her mind, was a thing of beauty—muscular from a life working on the ranch, with hard, sinewy muscle on his thighs, his arms and shoulders. He wasn't an extraordinarily tall man, but he was an extraordinarily well-built man.

"Do you like what you see?" Bruce asked her, standing unabashed in his nakedness.

Savannah moved to kneel before him in the water; her eyes drifted down to his erection, the proof of his desire for her.

"Yes." She reached for him. "I do."

Cupping him in her hands, she took him into her mouth, loving the sound of his groan, and the feel of his hands in her hair.

"That's going to get me in trouble," Bruce said in a tight voice.

As her lips left him, her hands stroked him. "Then hurry up and join me before the water gets cold."

Bruce stepped into the tub, sank down in the water behind her and then pulled her into his arms. Skin to slippery skin, her husband's strong fingers massaged her breasts while he kissed the water from her shoulder and neck.

"I have missed this—you have no idea," Bruce said in a raspy, strained tone, his hand slipping between her thighs to cover her slick center.

Savannah arched back, pushing into his hand. "Yes," she gasped, "I do."

She spun in his arms, sloshing water on the floor, and hovered above his body, her hands braced on his shoulders. Bruce wrapped his arms around her, hugging her to him, his mouth hot on her breast.

"I need you, Savannah." He grazed her nipple with his teeth. "I need you."

It was too long between moments for them; she sank

down, slipping him inside of her. A perfect fit—so thick and hard, he filled her completely.

With one arm, he lifted her forward, the water swirling around their bodies, so she could sit down completely and wrap her legs around his hips. Her moans mingled with his as their bodies melded together. She took his face in her hands, kissed his lips as he moved inside of her.

"Baby—I've got to come."

"It's okay." She held on to him as he bucked beneath her. "It's okay."

Bruce came with a loud growl, grabbing her shoulders and pulling her body down ono his. As he shuddered beneath her, catching his breath, she leaned into him, loving this moment in his arms.

"I'm sorry," he apologized. "I wanted it to last longer."

Savannah slipped her body free of his with a laugh, and echoed his words earlier. "Is the night over?"

That sexual glint returned to his eyes when he realized that she was ready and willing to go another round. "Not for me."

It was his pleasure to dry off his wife's body and carry her to bed. He laid her down, her skin still a little damp, and indulged Savannah, loving her with his mouth and his tongue, until she was arching her back, reaching for him and writhing with desire. It was the time his body needed to recover, to recharge and to harden. Bruce covered Savannah's body with his and joined them together once again. This time, he loved her slow and long, knowing her body as he knew his own, driving her to climax, one right after the other, until she was screaming and out of breath, their bodies slick with sweat.

They rolled together so Savannah was on top, straddling him, riding him, clawing his chest with her nails. He pulled her down on top of him, slowing them down, not wanting it to end.

"Are you coming for me, baby?"

He could feel her heart beating against his chest, her breath shallow, the little gasps of pleasure so satisfying. He forced himself to wait until he felt that familiar tensing of her legs, that sweet sound of her panting as she began her climb to the peak of another orgasm.

"Yes, baby—yes." Bruce held her tight and kissed her. "You're mine."

Seconds after Savannah peaked, he rolled her onto her back and pushed deep inside of her to find his own release.

The weeks that followed their second first date, their marriage had been a honeymoon state. They made love every chance they got, always taking the bed for themselves for lovemaking, before letting the canine family into the bedroom. They went out on more dates, going to the movies and out to dinner, trying new cuisine as they created a new foundation for their marriage. For Savannah, even though her memory still hadn't returned, remembering wasn't a high priority. Why would she want to go back to the reason why they split up when they were doing so well now? Why rock the boat?

"I'm so glad we could finally make our schedules work," Shayna Wade, a professor at Montana State University, and one of her longtime friends, told her.

"Me, too," Savannah agreed. Spending time with her family and friends had, day by day, made her feel very nearly like her old self—the self before the accident.

After they ordered their food, Shayna put her glass down and said, "I really wish you'd consider going back to school. I know you love being a teacher, but you always wanted to get your PhD. I'd love to have you on faculty with me."

"I'm not ruling it out."

"Good." Her friend seemed pleased with her answer.

"But right now, honestly, I'm just really focused on my therapy and my marriage."

"Your speech is so much better—you sound like you again."

"I've made a lot of progress," Savannah agreed with a smile. "I just want to keep on making progress."

They talked nonstop during lunch, catching up for the time that had lapsed since they last saw each other. After the plates were taken away and they were waiting for the bill, Shayna excused herself to the restroom while Savannah took the opportunity to answer emails and texts.

"Savannah."

A strange chill scurried down her spine; she looked up, and she could feel the blood drain from her face.

"Leroy." The word was said with a waver in her voice.

The cowboy's face brightened; without asking, he took a seat at the table. "You remember me?"

She looked around for Shayna, wishing that she could disappear into the woodwork.

"I…" She met his expectant eyes, so full of hope,

and gave a little shake of her head. "No. I'm sorry. I don't…remember you."

She remembered the lanky cowboy, who appeared to be younger than her, from the hospital, not from any memory before that time. But she did know that they had been dating and that it was his car she was driving when she had the accident.

"But—" his eyes shuttered "—you do know who I am."

Her hands gripped her phone to keep them from shaking. She nodded her response.

The young man's eyes were wet with emotion. "I love you, Savannah."

The only response Savannah could muster was, "I'm sorry."

Leroy stared at her for what seemed like several very long minutes before he coughed, cleared his throat and stood up. He looked down at the wedding ring back on her finger.

"One day you're gonna wake up and realize you're with the wrong man. I promise you, you're gonna remember that you want to marry me."

Those words hurt her heart, and no matter how much sympathy she felt for this man, and she did feel that sympathy, those were words she did not want to hear.

"No. I won't." She shook her head, her body shaking on the inside. "I'm already married."

Leroy turned away from her, almost bumping into Shayna in the process.

"Shayna." Leroy acknowledged her friend before he left the restaurant.

"Hi, Leroy." Shayna greeted the cowboy, then sat

down, a shocked expression on her face. "Are you okay?"

Savannah pulled some cash out of her wallet, handed it to her friend. "Will you take care of the bill? I need to go."

Chapter Eight

"How are things?" Dr. Kind asked her.

"I ran into Leroy yesterday," Savannah blurted out. She'd been keeping it bottled up inside for an entire day and she had been anxious to sit down and talk about it with the psychologist.

"And how did that feel?"

How did that *feel*?

"It felt terrible. The look on his face when I told him that I didn't remember him… He still loves me."

"Are you surprised by that? He hasn't forgotten your relationship."

"Well, I wish he would," Savannah snapped. "I don't want him to love me. I love Bruce. I'm married to Bruce."

"Yes," Dr. Kind agreed. "But you were in a relationship with Leroy. That's also true."

Savannah frowned. It was true—but she didn't *want* it to be the truth. She couldn't change the way she felt about that.

"So, how are things with your marriage?"

"We're in a really good place right now."

"Intimacy?"

"That couldn't be going any better." Savannah smiled. They had just made love that morning before Bruce left for a day of work on the ranch. She didn't want anything to spoil that momentum; losing it was one of her biggest fears.

Dr. Kind took some notes, then looked up thoughtfully. "Does it bother you that you haven't regained your memory?"

"No." She played with her wedding band. "Not like it used to. Why do I want to remember why I wanted to divorce my husband? We're happy right now—that's what matters to me."

"Do you think that's sustainable?"

"What do you mean?"

"Well," the psychologist said after a pause, "up until now, your world has been sanitized. Your friends and family have agreed, with your full knowledge, to protect you from that part of your past with Bruce that triggered the separation, and ultimately, the move to divorce."

It was true. Her friends and family had deleted digital traces of the past several years that might be emotionally upsetting to her. She was aware of it, and she hadn't gone out snooping to unearth images of the past several years. Was she being an ostrich and sticking her head in the sand? Yes. She was. But what was really wrong with that?

"So, I'll ask you again. Do you think this is sustainable? Leroy is just the first reminder of a past you have been actively avoiding. As you go back to work and live your life, pieces of that puzzle will continue to appear."

Savannah didn't have an immediate answer for the doctor, so she remained silent.

"Your body has healed from the accident. You've been cleared to ride horses again, and the neurologist has released you from his care. You have made great strides with both physical and speech therapy, and your marriage is also moving forward. The one place you are refusing to heal is your psychological and emotional health. Don't build your new life on a weak foundation, Savannah. Face what you need to face so you can truly move forward in your life and in your marriage."

"Hey." Bruce found Savannah in her garden at the end of the day. This little piece of ground had always been her salvation and her sanity. If she was having a bad day, if she was having a good day, it was always a day for getting her hands in the earth.

Savannah sat back on her haunches with a smile. "Hi!"

His wife had dirt on the tip of her nose and dirt on her chin. To him, it was adorable.

"Did you have a good day?"

"Uh-huh." She nodded. "I had a good session with Dr. Kind."

"Good."

Savannah stood up, brushed her hands off on her jeans and walked over to give him a hug. "I'm glad to see you."

He gave her a kiss. "I'm glad to see you."

Together, arm in arm, they went into the house, followed by the dogs, to get ready for dinner.

"I'm going to jump into the shower." Bruce shut the back door behind them. "Care to join me?"

Savannah laughed. "It's tempting. But no. I want to wash the veggies and get dinner started. Rain check?"

Bruce smiled at her with a wink. He was happy that the intimacy in their relationship was back and better than ever. They knew each other's bodies; they knew how to please each other. And that had been a big part of their connection as a couple—great lovemaking with your best friend. What could be better than that?

In the bedroom, Bruce picked up some of Savannah's discarded clothes and put them in the hamper along with his work clothes.

"You gonna hang with me, Hound Dog?" He scratched the dog around the scruff and kissed him on the head before he jumped in the shower.

After his shower, Bruce got dressed and was looking forward to a night at home with his wife. He was on the way out of the bedroom when something on the top of Savannah's dresser caught his eye. Something that made him stop in his tracks.

The rancher stared at the Matchbox fire truck— rusted in places, but still recognizable as the truck he had purchased what seemed like a lifetime ago. Bruce picked up the fire truck, memories, unwanted memories, flooding his mind. He clutched the truck in his hand, his eyes closed to push back the tears. It took him several minutes to gather his emotions; with the truck still in hand, Bruce went to find his wife in the kitchen.

"Could you watch this and stir it when it starts to

bubble? I seriously need a shower before we sit down to eat. I stink."

"Yeah. Sure." Bruce nodded, dropping a kiss on her lips as she walked by.

"Hey…"

Savannah spun around. "Huh?"

"Where did you find this?" He opened the palm of his hand to show her the fire truck.

"Oh!" She seemed to have forgotten all about it. "It was buried in the garden. It must've been Cole's, don't you think?"

The fact that Savannah had assumed that the truck had once belonged to Liam's son, his nephew Cole, told him everything he wanted to know. The truck hadn't triggered any memories for her.

He gave her a noncommittal nod, then tucked the toy into his pocket, and wondered how he was going to get through the night pretending that nothing was wrong.

"Damn." Bruce pinched the corners of his eyes to stop tears from forming. He would have thought that he had already cried out all of those tears years ago.

The night Bruce found the toy truck on Savannah's dresser, he didn't sleep. He tossed and turned, and only managed to drop off just before dawn. He awakened feeling hungover from lack of sleep and emotionally shell-shocked. Everything he had spent years suppressing, years avoiding, years ignoring, had suddenly bubbled up to the surface. Like Savannah, he was enjoying their marriage revival; he had his lover back—he had his best friend back. And the idea of rocking the boat by dredging up their past was something he didn't mind putting off.

That morning, Bruce kissed Savannah goodbye and headed off to meet his crew of ranch hands; that morning, he left with that toy fire truck in the front pocket of his jeans.

"I've got some things I've got to take care of in town," Bruce said to his brother Colton. "You good to keep the boys on track today?"

Colton was a die-hard Montana rancher like himself—Sugar Creek was his life.

"Not a problem." Colton gave him a nod.

Bruce climbed into his truck, shut the door and rolled down the window. Almost as an afterthought, he called out to Colton, who was striding toward the day's work.

"Hey, Colt."

Colton turned back to him.

"Go easy on Savannah tomorrow at breakfast. The two of you used to be real tight."

His younger brother's smile dropped. "She did you real wrong, brother. I'm just waitin' to see if she's gonna do it again. That's how I feel. That's how it's gonna be."

"She's still my wife," Bruce reminded him, before he shifted into Drive and drove through the field to pick up one of the many gravel roads that crisscrossed the ranch.

Colton was a carbon copy of Jock—he was passionate, demanding, driven to a fault, and could be unforgiving. While the rest of the family had found a way to make peace with Savannah's return to the ranch, Colt was a noticeable holdout.

Halfway down the main gravel road, Bruce turned onto a dirt road that was overgrown with tall grass.

This was truly a road less traveled on the ranch. His heart started to pound hard in his chest the farther down the road he drove; he felt nauseous as the family cemetery came into view. In Montana, families could still bury their kin on their land, as long as that land was outside of city limits and not near a water source. Jock's first wife, his mother, was the first person to be buried on Sugar Creek Ranch. Jock had already stipulated in his will that, when he was pushing up daisies, he wanted to be pushing up daisies on Sugar Creek.

Bruce shifted into Park and shut off the engine. He leaned his arms on the steering wheel, staring hard at the four headstones in the Brand plot. It took him some time to muster up the determination to get out of the truck and pick his way through the brush to where the unadorned headstones lined up in a row—one large headstone and three smaller headstones.

A wrought-iron fence surrounded the family plot; the stiff gate squeaked loudly as the rancher pushed it open. Slowly, reverently, Bruce walked over to the headstones and stared at the names and the dates carved into the granite markers. He silently acknowledged his mother, wishing now that he had come more often to clean the leaves and the debris off the headstones. The two little headstones next to his mother were his older twin brothers. His mother had nearly died when she miscarried twin boys before she carried him to term. But the headstone he was here to see was the third small marker.

Bruce knelt down next to the headstone—a headstone Savannah had picked out—and brushed dewdamp leaves and dirt off the granite marker. The name carved into the stone, along with the date of death, came into focus. Bruce dropped onto his knees; tears that refused to be ignored poured out of his eyes.

Samuel Jackson Brand.

Beloved Son.

A torrent of memories of the day that Savannah had watched him, along with his brothers, lower their two-year-old son into the ground, memories he had fought to forget, overwhelmed him.

"I'm so sorry, Sammy," Bruce said in a strangled voice.

This was why he had avoided this place—it was too hard. This was too hard.

Bruce took the toy truck out of his pocket and placed it on the top of the headstone. This had been one of his son's favorite toys; he deserved to have it returned to him.

The rancher rubbed the tears out of his eyes, then stood up. How could he even begin to tell Savannah about her son? How could he even begin to tell her that he was responsible for his death?

He left the place that had haunted him—stalked him in his waking moments as well as his dreams. Bruce didn't often feel like he needed advice; he usually knew his own mind. But when he needed counsel, there was one person he sought out, and that was his adoptive mother, Lilly.

He took his time driving back to the main house—he wanted to give himself time to get his emotions under control. When he reached the home he shared with Savannah, he noted that her truck was gone, which meant that she had already gone into town for physical therapy. He parked his truck at their cabin, let the dogs out of the house so they could join him on his walk to the main house.

Bruce found his mother, Lilly, in the sewing loft Jock had built for her. Lilly loved to watch the sun rise and set, so her loft was strategically placed to give her a year-round view of the sun rising in the east and setting in the west.

"Good morning, Mom."

His mother, a Scottish-born woman, had died when he was young; when Lilly came into his life and accepted him so completely as her own, over time, it had been natural for him to refer to his stepmother simply as Mom.

"Son." Lilly reached out her arms for a hug and gave him her usual kiss on the cheek.

Bruce pulled up a chair next to Lilly's workstation, which was stacked high with little plastic boxes of different colors and types of beads.

"What are you working on now?" he asked.

Lilly had always been devoted to her Chippewa-Cree heritage—she was proud of her lineage and was active with her tribe in the preservation of the language, ceremonies and traditions.

"Bracelets." His stepmom held up a bangle that she was hand beading with artistic patterns traditional to her tribe.

"You make beautiful things."

She smiled gently at the compliment. Lilly was a lovely woman who had aged gracefully; her skin, the color of dark golden honey, was finely lined on her forehead and around her eyes, but still held a youthful glow that defied her age. The only giveaways to her real age were the increasingly present strands of silver, which she refused to cover, that stood out in stark contrast to her raven-black hair.

"You're troubled," his mother observed, reading him so easily with her velvety brown eyes.

Lilly was an astute woman, sensitive, kind and insightful. Bruce often marveled at the match between her and Jock.

"I am," he admitted.

"I'm listening." Lilly put the partially beaded bracelet down and turned her body toward him.

Much like the day he had unloaded on Dr. Kind unexpectedly, Bruce unloaded on his mother. He didn't know how to move forward with Savannah without reopening a scabbed-over wound; he couldn't see a way forward in his marriage unless he went back first.

"Isn't it time for you to forgive yourself?" his mother asked him quietly, her eyes full of empathy.

Bruce swallowed hard to keep fresh tears at bay. "I don't even know where to begin."

And if he couldn't forgive himself, how could he expect Savannah to forgive him? She hadn't been able to forgive him the first time around—what would be different now?

"Yes, you do," she disagreed. "You have always known."

These words were followed by a moment of silence. Then, his mother said, "What was once broken has healed back stronger for the breaking."

His mother often spoke in riddles, and he wished she could just talk in a straight line sometimes.

"You are stronger now as a couple. I see you together. This time will be different." She elaborated. "Trust what you feel. Trust that you can weather this storm—together this time—instead of letting it rip you apart.

"It's time, son." Lilly put both of her hands over his. "It's time to tell Savannah what her mind has forgotten."

After Sunday breakfast at the main house with the family, Savannah couldn't wait to go to the barn and saddle up. Now that she was cleared to ride again, trail riding up to one of the mountain peaks that abutted Sugar Creek was top on her list for their Sunday date. Even Colton's surly mood toward her when she bumped into him in the tack room didn't dampen her happiness.

They saddled two of the ranch's quarter horses and set out together. Up the narrow trail, she took the lead, loving the scent of the wildflowers growing unbidden along the path, and reveling in the feel of the light breeze cooling her face. This was what she had been missing so much; she was so grateful to spend this beautiful day, on horseback, with her husband.

"There's a good spot to dismount up ahead," she called over her shoulder to Bruce.

They were going to have to lead the horses on foot at the narrowest part of the trail just before they reached the peak. At a safe area for her and her horse, Savannah swung her leg over the animal's back and dropped down to the ground. She slipped the reins over her mount's head and gave the horse an affectionate pat on the neck while she waited for Bruce to follow suit.

"We couldn't have a better day for this." Her husband joined her.

She beamed up at him. "I know. It's the most beautiful day we've had all summer."

Bruce looked at her with so much love, so much appreciation, that it warmed her on the inside of her body just as the sun was warming the outside.

"It makes me happy to see you so happy," he said before he leaned down to kiss her lips.

"Being here with you. That makes me happy."

They led the horses single file along the narrow trail; on either side of the path, dangerous, rocky slopes made Savannah cautious with every step.

"I think this is as far as the horses should go." Bruce had taken the lead on this leg of the journey.

They tied the horses with breakaway knots and then carefully climbed their way to the peak of the mountain. There was a favorite spot—their spot—where they would sit together and take in the view spread out before them. On a clear day, they could see for miles.

At the top, a large boulder jutted out from the side of the mountain. This was the target. Savannah loved to sit on that boulder and dangle her legs over the edge. It was like a natural diving board thousands of feet in the air.

"Careful." Bruce held on to her hand as she sat down.

Her husband sat next to her, thigh to thigh, arms intertwined.

"Just look at this, Bruce." Savannah sighed. "It's heaven on earth."

"Yes, it is."

Savannah rested her head on her husband's shoulder, feeling happier in this moment than she could remember.

"I love you." She looked at his strong, hawkish profile.

Bruce leaned over and kissed her lightly on the lips. "I love you more."

Chapter Nine

Their Sunday ended with a quiet dinner that they prepared together, and a movie at home. They didn't see the end of the movie—instead, they let the dogs take over the couch while they went into the bedroom to make love. Sometimes, their lovemaking was hot and aggressive, and other times, Bruce liked to love her slowly, sensually. Either way, it was always passionate.

Naked in the moonlight, Savannah waited for her husband to join her. An unclothed Bruce Brand was a thing of beauty—so muscular and masculine.

"I wish I could take your picture right now." Bruce stopped at the edge of the bed. "You look so sexy."

She smiled at him. "I'm glad you think so."

Bruce started at her feet, dropping butterfly kisses on her ankles, her calves, the inside of her thighs. Savannah moaned with pleasure when he began to kiss that most sensitive spot between her thighs. She threaded her fingers into his hair, and her head dropped back onto the pillow. It didn't take long for her body to want more—to be closer to Bruce, to feel his naked skin against hers, to feel his body fill hers so completely, so perfectly.

With a frustrated little noise in the back of her throat, Savannah let her husband know that she was ready for him. Always responsive to her needs, Bruce dropped a last kiss on her mound before he covered her body with his. She gasped as he slipped inside her, joining their bodies together; he pushed himself up, locking his elbows so he could watch her as he loved her. Savannah held on to his arms, loving the feel of the hard muscles beneath her fingertips, just as she loved the feel of his rock-hard erection moving inside of her.

Every move Bruce made was slow and deliberate— he wanted to have the control, and she was happy to let him. Savannah gasped again, lifted her knees so he could go deeper, take longer strokes as her fingernails dug into his arm.

"Open your eyes," he said in a lover's tender voice.

Savannah opened her eyes for a split second, before she had to close them again as an orgasm forced her to arch her back and lift her hips to take him ever deeper still inside of her.

As she shuddered beneath him, her eyes still closed, her lips parted, Bruce kissed her breasts, her neck, before he wrapped his arms around her and rolled them both to their sides. Her legs were enfolded around his body; she opened her eyes to find him staring at her face.

"How was that?" he asked with a pleased smile.

"Incredible." She took his face in her hands and kissed his lips. "Absolutely incredible."

He ran his hand down her hip, gripped her derriere and pulled her body closer into his.

"Hmm," she murmured. "You feel so good."

Their arms and legs intertwined, Savannah buried her face in Bruce's neck, breathing in that wonderful, familiar scent of his skin. They made love to each other again, their bodies pressed tightly together, their hips falling into a sensual rhythm. By the time her handsome husband growled out a loud, throaty climax that seemed to come from somewhere deep in his soul, they were both drenched in sweat, breathless, hugging each other, and sighing with postcoital satisfaction.

Bruce lay on his back, his chest rising and falling as he caught his breath. He gave a little laugh. "We have always been so very good at that."

Savannah pushed her damp hair off her forehead before she lay down on her back beside him, using his arm as a pillow.

"We really have," she agreed with a smile. "Making love with you just keeps on getting better. I bet we'll still be humping like rabbits when we're in our eighties."

"God willing."

They let their three canine family members into the bedroom and took a quick shower and got ready for bed. Savannah was the first human in bed, while the entire bottom part of the mattress was covered in layers of dogs.

"Really, guys?" Savannah reached forward to pet each animal. "Where am I supposed to put my feet?"

Bruce closed the door behind him and climbed into

bed beside her. He loved to spoon her, wrapping her up in his arms as if she were a giant, cuddly teddy bear. Some nights she was too warm to be cocooned by her husband's usually hot skin, but tonight she couldn't think of another way she'd rather drift off to sleep.

"Comfortable?" Bruce's nose was buried in her hair.

"Uh-huh."

"Good night, sugar."

"'Night." She loved the way her husband smelled right out of the shower. "I love you."

He pulled her even closer to his body and kissed the back of her neck. "I love you more."

One of life's little pleasures on the ranch was to be able to observe her husband from the front porch. She would curl up on one of the two-seater chairs with the dogs and watch her husband do what he loved to do… working in his workshop across the way, or mowing the grass around the house, or fixing fences for the surrounding pastures. Her husband was a Montana rancher to his core, and she loved that about him. She, on the other hand, loved being a Montana woman, born and bred, but she'd had a lot to learn about being married to a rancher at the beginning of her marriage.

Bruce saw her on the porch, said something to the men he had been working with, and then headed her way. His T-shirt was soaked with sweat—on his chest, his stomach and under his arms. For her, Bruce was the most handsome man on the planet. How lucky had she gotten to marry a family-oriented, kind, loyal, sexy cowboy like Bruce Brand? There was a part of her, perhaps more than she was willing to acknowledge, that *wanted* to know what had led to the divorce. But the part of her that didn't want to rock the boat, that didn't want to ruin what was so good with her husband now, was the part that won out time and again. Savannah knew it was wrong, yet she just didn't trust that the tenuous bond she had forged with Bruce could weather the truth.

"Make some room, guys," her husband said to the dogs surrounding her.

Buckley moved so Bruce could sit down on a small sliver of the chair.

"How's it going?" she asked, handing him her glass of sweet tea.

"It's slow goin'," the rancher said before he gulped down the rest of her tea. "But we're getting there."

They sat in silence for several minutes, comfortable in those moments when neither spoke.

"I thought your sister was coming out today."

"She woke up feeling like she was catching a cold."

Her husband nodded, putting the empty glass on the ground next to the chair.

"The vet sent a reminder email." She rubbed the top of Hound Dog's head, lifting up his ears and scratching him around the neck. "It's time to take the gang in for their shots."

Bruce nodded again and looked as if he was going to get up and go back to work.

"Hey." Savannah turned her body toward him a bit. "I've been wanting to tell you something."

"What's that?"

She hated bringing up Leroy—to her, there was this open wound that was trying to heal, and bringing up the topic of a man she'd been dating while they were going through the divorce was like rubbing dirt in the wound. But she had to tell Bruce; she had put it off long enough.

"You know I went out to lunch with Shayna the other day?"

He nodded to let her know that he was listening, but his attention was on his phone and scrolling through texts and emails.

She poked him on the leg with her foot. "Would you put that down for a second, please? This is important."

He tucked the phone back into the pocket of his T-shirt, then looked at her.

"Thank you." Savannah gave a little shake of her head—Bruce had become increasingly addicted to that phone to the point of being annoying. "I don't even know how to bring this up with you, so I'm just going to tell you. Leroy was at the restaurant."

Bruce stared at her for a second, then looked away. "How was that?"

"Horrible."

Her husband looked back as she continued.

"I don't remember him, or at least I don't remember my relationship with him." She crossed her arms in front of her body. "I know he wants me to remember so…"

"…you'll go back to him." The muscle in Bruce's cheek jumped from him clenching his jaw.

He was right—she knew he was right. And it hurt. "I'm glad I don't remember him. I don't *want* to remember."

Savannah had to tell herself not to hold her breath as she stared at her husband's profile. Neither of them wanted to have these conversations; it reminded them that, even though their marriage seemed to be back on track, it wasn't always that way.

Bruce stood up, his eyes shuttered. "I've got to get back to it."

"Okay." She felt sick in her stomach.

He was on his way down the steps when she stopped him. "Hey—where's my kiss, Brand?"

The rancher stopped, turned and pushed the brim of his cowboy hat up with one finger. Wordlessly, he returned to her, bent down and kissed her on the lips.

Savannah grabbed his fingers and held on. "We can't shut down on each other."

"You're right," he agreed with her. "That's not going to help."

Bruce returned to work, swallowing back acid that had started to churn in his stomach the minute Leroy's name came out of his wife's mouth. During the separation and the divorce process, whenever Savannah had talked about Leroy, or he saw the two of them in town holding hands, he wanted to punch the young cowboy in the throat. He knew that Savannah hadn't recovered any of those memories of her relationship with Leroy, but he remembered it all too well. To see his wife, a woman he still very much loved, with another man had made him feel helpless and furious. He'd often found it hard to concentrate on his work or sleep thinking about them. And hearing Leroy's name come out of Savannah's mouth unearthed all of those feelings he had been trying to bury for the sake of salvaging his marriage.

He threw himself into work, the familiar routine of replacing fence boards, a task that relied on muscle memory rather than thinking, giving him a chance to ponder his mother's advice. The relationship between Savannah and himself, on the surface at least, seemed to be stronger than ever, yet he felt like he was standing on shifting sand. Just as Savannah had been worried about telling him about her innocent encounter with Leroy, he too had been worried about opening a Pandora's box by discussing the tragedy that had led to their separation in the first place.

"Coward," Bruce muttered to himself, unmindful of the fact that his brother could hear him.

"What was that?" Colton was a couple of feet down the line, yanking on a stubborn board that wouldn't dislodge from the fence post.

"Nothing," he dodged. Colton, of all people, was the last person he wanted to talk to about his marriage.

But it wasn't "nothing"; he was being a coward. He and Savannah couldn't live in this fantasy bubble forever. They needed to face their past, and because Savannah was happy to leave it "forgotten," Bruce knew that they were heading for trouble. Their past—their mutual tragedy—couldn't be avoided forever. It was inevitable—one day, someone was going to mention Sammy to Savannah. It was just a matter of time, and he couldn't allow that to happen.

He had to be the one to tell Savannah about her son; he had to be the one to tell her about their dear, sweet baby boy, Sammy.

Bruce cut out of work early; he knew that he couldn't spend one more night with his wife without making a plan to face their past. He wasn't sure how to best tackle the subject. Should they be with Dr. Kind? Should they be with Savannah's family? Or should this be a private moment between husband and wife? If there was a right way to handle this, he sure as heck didn't know what it was.

He walked through the door, expecting to be greeted with music and the scent of something cooking in the kitchen. Savannah was on a cooking jag, of which he had been a happy beneficiary. But as he shut the door behind him, greeted by his three faithful dogs, the feeling in the house was off. It was quiet—no music playing—and the kitchen was empty and cold.

Bruce put his hat on the hook, showed each dog some attention, before he called out to his wife. That sick feeling returned to his stomach when Savannah didn't respond. He followed the dogs down the hallway toward the bedroom; he found his wife in the office, sitting at his desk, with an enlarged picture of Sammy in Savannah's lap, his chubby arms around her neck. They were both smiling so broadly, so happy to be with each other; in the picture, Savannah's eyes were sparkling with joy at the simple pleasure of holding their son in her arms.

Fear, pure, stripped-down fear, sent a cold shiver across his body. His heart was pounding, and he was stuck in his spot, unable to speak, unable to move.

Savannah turned in the swivel chair so she could face him.

"Who is this little boy?" she asked him. He could tell by the confusion in her eyes that she recognized that this child in the picture was someone important, but she couldn't remember why. This moment was exactly what he had feared—now there wasn't any way to break the news gently to Savannah. The bandage had just been ripped off without any finesse to minimize the pain she would assuredly feel.

"Samuel." Bruce had to swallow several times before he was able to say his son's name out loud to Savannah after so many years. "Our son, Samuel."

Why she had picked that day to be curious, Savannah couldn't figure. She had sat down at the computer to find a recipe for dinner, but had decided to click on the photo album instead. Bruce had never hidden the photo album—there wasn't a password lock on the computer. She could have looked at the pictures at any time. Until now—until today—she hadn't wanted to look. It had been her choice.

Savannah felt the color drain from her face, felt her stomach clench, when Bruce said the name "Samuel." Somewhere, deep in the forgotten memories of her mind, that name reverberated in the tissue of her body—that name reverberated in her soul.

"Our son..."

She turned back to the picture, one of the few she had found featuring this little boy. Savannah reached out and touched the screen with her fingertips. In a whisper, she said, "We called him Sammy."

"Yes." Bruce's voice sounded choked. "We did. Do you...remember him?"

Savannah pressed her hand to her mouth, the salty taste of her fresh tears on her tongue. She shook her head again and again, unable to speak. All she could think was "our son" over and over, trying to make sense of it. Trying to understand.

"Where is he?" she asked, her voice muffled behind her hand. "Why isn't he here with us?"

When Bruce didn't respond right away, Savannah stood up, her face wet with tears pouring from her stricken eyes.

She put her hand on her heart. "How can I not know that I have a *son*? How can I not *know* this?"

He crossed the divide between them, pulled her into his arms, ignoring her resistance, wrapped her in his arms, his chin on the top of her head.

"Where is my son?" Savannah demanded, her tears wetting the front of Bruce's shirt. *"Why isn't he here with us?"*

As if he wanted to stop her from running away from him, her husband tightened his grip on her body. And then he said the words she knew were coming—she couldn't remember it, but she could *feel* it, in her heart, in her gut.

"God, please help me say it." She felt Bruce's tears fall into her hair. "He died, Savannah. Our son's gone."

Savannah pushed on his chest and twisted her body to make him let her go. She backed away from her husband; the shock and pain and horror felt like a knife slicing at her skin. No words… No words… There were no words.

With a moan of anguish, Savannah pushed past her husband and ran to the bathroom. She slammed the door shut behind her, locked it, and then landed on her knees in front of the commode, retching. Clutching her stomach, she flushed the toilet and stumbled to the sink. The water was ice-cold from the faucet— she rinsed out her mouth and washed the tears from her face.

"Savannah." Bruce knocked on the door and rattled the knob. "Please, let me in."

"Go away," she told him in a raspy voice.

She had a son—a darling little boy with her dimples and Bruce's incredible blue eyes. And she couldn't *remember him*. He had been erased from her brain—erased from her life; it was a cruelty that she couldn't handle. It was a cruelty she couldn't comprehend.

Why can't I remember? How could I not have known?

Savannah stared at her reflection in the mirror—her cheeks and her nose were red, her eyes bloodshot with puffy lids. She put her hands on her breasts—they had changed; she had noticed that. They were a little larger, a little saggier, but it had never occurred to her that it was anything more than fluctuating weight and gravity. Had Samuel suckled them? Had she breastfed her son even though she had never been interested in breastfeeding?

Still looking at her reflection, Savannah lifted up her shirt and pushed down the waistband of her jeans. There were some stretch marks on her stomach, on her hips—hairline, barely noticeable, white marks on her skin. Her hands pressed into her abdomen; she had gotten pregnant, carried a child, given birth to a child, and held that child in her arms. She knew that now. But she couldn't remember the scent of his skin; she couldn't remember what it felt like to hold that chubby body in her arms.

"What kind of mother would forget her own son?" Savannah frowned at her reflection with the smallest shake of the head.

"Savannah." Bruce's voice cut through the door and cut through her own dark thoughts. "Let me in."

All of the emotions she had been feeling seemed

to be pulled out of her body, leaving a gaping, empty, numb hole in their place. Slowly, stiffly, like a robot, Savannah unlocked the bathroom door, turned the handle, and pulled the door open.

On the other side of the door, her husband and her dogs waited for her. Hound Dog was whimpering, his worried eyes on her face. They were so intuitive; they knew, without understanding the words, that something was very wrong in their house.

"Savannah." Her husband's face was ashen. "I'm so sorry. There was no easy way…"

She slipped past him, wordlessly, and went to the kitchen. There, she picked up her keys, her phone and her wallet.

"Where are you going?"

Savannah had trouble looking at him, so instead she looked past him. "I need time."

She was hurting him—she saw the pain in his eyes in her peripheral vision—but she couldn't handle his pain right now. Not right now.

"You said that we can't shut each other out." For the first time, Bruce sounded angry. "That's what you said not two hours ago."

Now she looked him directly in the eyes, her own anger bubbling to the top like magma bubbling up from a volcano. "You don't have a right to dictate how I feel or how I react to this, Bruce. Do you get that? You don't have the *right*."

Chapter Ten

The very thing he was afraid of had indeed come home to roost. He had waited too long to tell her, to soften the blow of Savannah finding out about their son. Perhaps he had hoped, in a way, that her memories of sweet Sammy would return on their own, saving him from the horrible task of telling Savannah that she was a mother and that their son was gone.

Watching his wife leave their home was reliving a scene from his past that he had suppressed for so long. Savannah had walked out on him before, and he hadn't put up a fight. He had been too emotionally raw himself, drowning in his own guilt, that he hadn't believed that he had a right to fight for his marriage. But this time, he was going to be different. He was going to put up one hell of a fight for his marriage.

He spent several hours reaching out to Savannah's

parents, her sisters and her friends. None of them had heard from her, but they all promised to call him right away if they did. It was a relief to have all of them on his side—this time around.

Bruce called her phone, sent her texts, tried to reach her by video chat. Savannah could be stubborn to a fault, and he finally had to accept that he would have to wait for her to return to him in her own way, in her own time. Tired of pacing, tired of not being able to concentrate on any one thing, Bruce finally decided to take a seat on the porch and wait for his wife to come home.

Somewhere along the way, he had fallen asleep on the porch. The sound of the dogs barking excitedly awakened him; he squinted at the early-morning sun and winced at the stiffness of his neck from sleeping upright all night.

The dogs were barking their greeting to Savannah. Bruce watched as his wayward wife parked the truck and got out. She reached down to pet the dogs, but her eyes were on him. Slowly, deliberately, Savannah crossed to the porch. At the bottom of the stairs, she stopped, her arms crossed tightly in front of her body.

"Hi." She had dark circles under her puffy red eyes.

"I'm glad you're back," he told her.

"I'm sorry I left like I did." She apologized in a quiet voice. "You didn't deserve that."

He appreciated the apology, but all he wanted was for her to stay this time—to work through the loss of their son together, something they hadn't been able to do before.

"I'm sorry." He stood up; he wanted so badly to take her in his arms, to hold her, to comfort her. But he was afraid of being pushed away. "I thought—we

all thought—that you needed time to heal before…"
His voice trailed off. Would it always be hard to say
his son's name out loud?

She leaned against the handrail on the stairs, arms
still crossed. "I drove around all night, trying to remember…trying to remember."

Savannah met his eyes, her own eyes damp with a
fresh cycle of tears. "I couldn't remember anything.
Not one thing."

Her next words broke his heart. "Will you…" She
stopped, cleared her throat, and then continued. "Will
you please tell me about our son?"

She waited on the couch, surrounded by her dogs,
while Bruce got his laptop from the bedroom. All night
she had tried to remember her son, but she couldn't.
She couldn't. Her brain had betrayed her, robbed her
of the precious memories of her only child. Now, she
needed to be strong enough to find out about her son's
life—and his death.

"Oh…" Savannah's fingers went up to her lips when
Bruce handed her pictures of her ultrasound. "Look
at him."

Bruce joined her, sitting next to her, but not touching her.

"You were so happy that day. We found out Sammy
was a Samuel instead of a Samantha."

Savannah ran her fingertips over the picture, touching her son's cheek. "He's sucking his thumb."

Bruce cracked a fleeting smile. "In the womb and
out of the womb. We couldn't keep his thumb out of
his mouth. Or his toes, for that matter."

She knew there would be more tears—how could

there not be? She held on to the ultrasound pictures with one hand and wiped the tears from her eyes with the other.

Her husband turned on the laptop; folder after folder was filled with a treasure trove of pictures featuring their son, Samuel Jackson Brand.

"How in the world did you talk me into the name?" Savannah mused aloud. Samuel L. Jackson was Bruce's favorite actor; he'd watched every Samuel L. Jackson movie at least twice.

"It took some doing," Bruce acknowledged. "But you loved it."

Picture after picture, Savannah began to create a three dimensional image of her son in her mind. He was a happy boy, full of energy and curiosity. He had loved all animals and anything with four wheels. Sammy had been an affectionate boy, always hugging someone in the pictures. And that smile—those dimples. He had been…perfect.

Bruce told her about the day they found out she was pregnant—it was a happy accident, an unplanned pregnancy with a rare but possible failure with the birth control pill. They had always wanted a family, but she'd wanted to wait until after she got settled in her career and decided to pursue a doctoral degree. He told her about the day their son was born; she had gone into labor three weeks early on a frosty fall morning. Bruce laughed a little when he recounted how they could see their breath while they were sniping at each other as they loaded into the truck to go to the hospital. He showed her the first pictures of her holding premature Sammy, his tiny pink body curled up on her chest as she smiled, with tired eyes and mussed hair, at the camera.

"I got it," Bruce told her. "Right then, what parents were always talking about. I had no idea how much I could love someone until I first met Sammy."

"I look so happy. In every picture with him. I look so happy."

"You took to motherhood. I think we were both shocked at how much you loved it." Bruce glanced over at her. "You kept on talking about how you wanted ten more just like him. Ten more."

She had so many questions, and he answered every one. Except for the biggest question of all—the one she was afraid to ask.

"Do you need a break?" her husband asked her when she stopped commenting on the pictures.

"No," she said faintly. "No. I don't. I need to know what happened."

Bruce closed the laptop and turned his head away from her.

"Sammy is gone because of me," he told her in a harsh whisper. "I'm to blame."

Savannah became a voracious consumer of home videos featuring her son—from the birth, which she couldn't believe she let Bruce videotape, but now was glad for it, to Samuel's first birthday party and so many more moments, both large and small, of her son's life. She knew his smile now; she knew the sound of his voice, the wonder that always seemed to be present in his wide, bright blue eyes. But she didn't know what it was like to tuck him into bed; she didn't know what it was like to feel his kiss on her cheek. And there was a possibility that her memory would never return, and her only connection with her son was one-dimensional.

That night, Savannah crawled into bed exhausted. She hadn't slept the night before, and the entire day had been spent trying to download every recorded second of her son's life into her brain. Bruce had been able to talk at length about their son's life—but he wasn't able to talk to her about his death. It was as if the words were stuck somewhere deep inside, and he just couldn't get them out. Maybe that was for the best. Maybe she needed some time to reflect on Sammy's beautiful life before she started to mourn the tragedy of his death. So she hadn't pushed Bruce. She didn't push him.

Bruce had stayed up long after she had turned in; when she felt the weight of her husband getting into his side of the bed, Savannah rolled over onto her back. As much has she had tried to fall asleep—as tired as she was—sleep escaped her. And what made it worse was that already they were shutting down, both of them. They hadn't told each other that they loved each other—and even though she obviously still felt it, she couldn't find her way to say the words out loud. It was so easy to see, so easy to understand, why they had ended up separating. Sammy's life had been such a source of joy and bonding between them; losing him had broken them apart.

"Bruce." She could tell by his breathing that he was still awake.

"Yes?"

You have to say the words, Savannah. Say the words.

"I love you."

After a moment of silence, not turning toward her, Bruce said in a clear voice, "I love you more."

Savannah reached out to touch her husband's back. "Will you take me to see Sammy tomorrow?"

Three full heartbeats of silence, and then Bruce said simply, "Yes."

For the second time in a very short time, Bruce returned to the family cemetery. He had worked very hard to push this place out of his mind, to shove aside the emotions attached to the place of his son's final resting place—but the truth was, this little plot of land, with its small marble headstone, was never far from his waking thoughts. The image of it had lurked in the background, haunting him.

"Your parents weren't so sure about burying Sammy here." Bruce shut off the engine. "But we both wanted him to be close. Sammy loved Sugar Creek. Even as young as he was, I could see that this ranch was in his blood."

They met at the front of the truck, and to his surprise, Savannah reached for his hand. Did he deserve this kindness? He didn't think so. But he was grateful for it. Together, hand in hand, they walked on the overgrown path the short distance to the plot of land surrounded by the black wrought-iron fence. They didn't say anything as they made their way over to Samuel's grave, but Savannah gasped when she saw the fire truck that she had found in the garden.

His wife dropped to her knees next to their son's headstone, her finger lightly tracing his name etched into the white marble.

"'Samuel Jackson Brand. Beloved son.'" Savannah read the simple wording on the grave. She had selected the headstone, the font style and the modest wording.

Seeing his wife on her knees beside their son's grave was more than Bruce could stand. He turned away, tears in his eyes, and walked back to the truck. How could he expect Savannah to forgive him if he couldn't find a way to forgive himself? Bruce climbed behind the wheel of his truck and watched Savannah through the windshield. She deserved to take as much time as she needed, to have this private moment at her son's graveside.

The pain he saw in his wife's eyes was the pain he felt in every layer of his body; it never really faded. That sorrow was a pain he had just had to learn to live with; now Savannah would have to learn to live with it again, too.

When Savannah finally stood up and started to walk back to the truck, Bruce hopped out and met her at the passenger-side door. He held the door open for her, his eyes sweeping her face. Her pretty oval face, a face he knew well and loved so much, was wet with freshly shed tears. He took a cloth handkerchief out of the back pocket of his jeans and handed it to her before he gently shut the door.

Savannah was blowing her nose loudly as he got back behind the wheel. He didn't start the engine; he just sat there, staring at their son's headstone.

"I only left him for a minute," Bruce said, still staring straight ahead, not wanting to look at his wife's face. "I promise you—it was only a minute."

Out of the corner of his eye, he saw Savannah watching him, hanging on his next words.

"But one minute was too long," he said with self-recrimination. "One second would have been too long."

Savannah put her hand on his leg, and this show of compassion, this show of support, gave him the strength to continue.

"You were in Tennessee visiting your sister," Bruce told her. "And I was going to spend some quality time with the little man." He laughed a hollow laugh. "I couldn't wait to spend that time with Sammy—I had so many plans. So many plans."

Bruce swallowed hard, choking back tears. "Right before we went to the airport, you told me that you had washed the towels, and all I had to do was get them out of the dryer, fold them and put them away in the bathroom."

He shook his head in disgust. "I have looked back at that moment a million times; why didn't I just take the towels out of the dryer when I got home? What was so important that made me put it off?"

Savannah's hand tightened on his leg.

"That day, I took him to the creek and he chased minnows for an hour. A whole hour. I can remember so clearly how loud he was laughing, stomping his feet in the water, trying to catch those little minnows with his chubby hands."

He glanced at Savannah, who had turned her body toward his. "Sammy loved water. Even when he was a baby, we never had to fight with him to get him into the bath. It was no different that night…" His voice trailed off as the memories, beautiful and horrible, came flooding back to him. "I put him in the tub for his bath that night. I remember he was excited about the new tugboat toy you had gotten for him. We played until that poor kid was all wrinkly from being in the water for too long…"

"But when I opened the cabinet to get a towel—" Bruce's voice cracked on the words, and he sniffed loudly. "I only left him for a minute. Just one minute."

"Oh, no." Savannah gasped as she put the missing, unspoken pieces in place. "No."

He couldn't say the words, "Sammy drowned." He just couldn't. It was his fault that their son was gone—accident or not. If he had just gotten the damn towels out of the dryer before he put Sammy in the tub—their son would still be alive. Their son would still be with them, and they would have never separated, they would have never gone through a divorce, and she would have never been with Leroy.

Savannah didn't yell at him or accuse him. Instead, she moved onto his lap, wrapped her arms around him and held him tightly while years of anger and self-loathing and sorrow poured out of him.

"I'm so sorry, Sammy…" he repeated over and over again. "I'm so sorry."

Bruce held on to Savannah, hugging her nearly breathless, as they wept together, mourning the loss of their precious son for the first time together. After they'd buried Samuel, Savannah had stopped touching him; she'd stopped sleeping in their bed. And, on his part, he didn't want to talk about Sammy. It was too painful. Unlike Savannah, who'd spent hours sitting on Sammy's brand-new "big boy" toddler bed, clutching his favorite stuffed toy to her chest, he'd wanted to strip the room and lock the door. Their grief took them down different roads; their grief had ended their marriage. Only time would tell if their son's tragic death would rip them apart again.

That night, they made love for the first time since she'd found the picture of Samuel. It was a quiet, poignant expression of their love, slow and tender. They held each other, kissed deeply and lingeringly, and mingled breath and sweet words of love. Savannah understood now *why* they had separated and eventually filed for divorce. One of her many flaws was her inability to forgive; she held herself and everyone else to very high standards, and this often led her to fail to forgive flaws in herself as well as others. She had turned her back on Bruce. At the time when he needed her the most—when he needed her to be his best friend and wife—she had walked away.

Yes, it was Bruce's terrible misjudgment that had resulted in their son's death. But wasn't she also culpable? Had she shown her husband some compassion, their marriage would have survived. And she would never have ended up in Leroy's muscle car the night of the crash.

The next day, they went to see their therapist together.

"I'm glad to see the both of you." Dr. Kind gestured for them to take a seat.

They had made an appointment with the psychologist; neither one of them wanted to see their marriage implode as it had before. Bruce didn't hesitate to agree to go back to see Dr. Kind. This was a signal to Savannah that Bruce was "all-in" with their marriage, and that gave her the strength to tackle her emotions around the death of her son without destroying her relationship with Bruce.

"So, where would you like to start today?"

This time, they were sitting side by side on the couch, which was an improvement from the last time they had sat on this sofa together.

"Do you want me to start?" she asked her husband.

He nodded, so she filled the psychologist in on the events of the last week—learning that she was a mother, and that her son had drowned on her husband's watch.

"That's a lot to learn," Dr. Kind noted. "And a lot for you, Bruce, to relive."

They both nodded. It was, in truth, more pain than any couple should have to endure.

"And how do you feel, Savannah, now that you know the truth?"

Savannah hesitated. "I feel…everything. Depressed, furious, cheated, guilty…"

"Let's explore the guilt," Dr. Kind said "What do you feel guilty about?"

"The divorce."

"That wasn't your fault," Bruce objected. "We both had our fingerprints all over that."

"Has any of this jarred memories for you, Savannah?"

"I remembered that we called Samuel 'Sammy.' I remembered his favorite stuffed animal. But that's all…"

"How did Savannah behave toward you after Samuel's death?" the psychologist asked Bruce.

Bruce didn't answer right away; Savannah gave his arm a little shake. "It's okay. You can tell me. That's why we're here."

Her husband swallowed hard, his hand clammier to the touch. Then, he cleared his throat and said, "She stopped loving me."

To hear Bruce say that she had stopped loving him had left her temporarily speechless and stunned. He hadn't said it to hurt her; he hadn't said it to be mean or vindictive. He had said it because that was how she had made him feel when she stopped kissing him, stopped holding his hand, stopped making love. She was certain that she never stopped loving Bruce. Not when she had left their marital bed, not when she had moved out, not when she had gotten involved with uncomplicated Leroy, and not when she had filed for divorce.

"I'm sorry, Bruce," she said on the drive back to the ranch.

"You don't owe me an apology."

"Yes, I do," Savannah was quick to say. "I left you when you needed me the most."

"I think there's a whole lot of people in this world who would think that you had all the reason in the world to leave me."

Savannah reached out her hand; Bruce switched hands on the steering wheel so he could take it.

"Maybe so. But they'd be wrong."

Chapter Eleven

That was the first of many sessions that the two of them had with Dr. Kind. It wasn't always easy, and they weren't always happy with each other when they left a session, but they were talking—and they were still together, and that was the goal.

Savannah flopped down on the couch next to Bruce, and tucked her feet beneath her.

"I've decided something," she announced.

As usual, Bruce was immersed in his phone, playing a game—the man was obsessed. Savannah put her hand over her husband's phone and pushed it down.

"I've made a decision."

Bruce never liked it when she covered the screen of his phone. "I was listening."

"I want you to *look* at me."

"Fine. I'm listening." Her husband put his phone

facedown on his leg and opened his eyes really wide as he stared at her. "*And* looking."

"I hope it's not too painful."

"It's never painful looking at you." He winked at her and leaned close so she'd kiss him.

She obliged, giving him a little kiss on the lips.

"So what have you decided?"

"Well," she said excitedly. "I've decided to get a tattoo."

He looked at her like she'd grown two horns and buck teeth.

"Why would you do that?"

Savannah shifted and then hooked her arm around her bent knee. "For Samuel. I want to get a portrait of him on my back." She reached over her right shoulder. "Right here."

It took her husband a short time to get onboard. "If that's what you want, I support you."

Savannah was pleased. "Good. Because I was going to do it either way."

Later that day, armed with the first picture of Sammy she had found on Bruce's computer, Savannah met her sister Justine, her sister-in-law, Jessie, and her friend Shayna at A Touch of Ink Tattoo parlor near the university in downtown Bozeman.

"Isabella is the best tattoo artist *ever*, trust me." Jessie's long, raven's-wing hair swung behind her as she walked with a youthful jaunt.

"Mom and Dad are going to have a baby cow." Justine repeated what she had been telling her sister for a week.

"It's my skin." Savannah loved her parents, but it was her body and her choice to honor her son in this way.

"I would love to get a tattoo," Shayna admitted.

"Get one with me!"

Shayna, a plus-size woman who always dressed in stylish but conservative clothing, shook her head no. "I'm not ready. But I wanted to be here to support you. I love the idea of keeping Samuel with you always."

Savannah felt elated at finally walking into the tattoo parlor, putting her plan into action.

"Welcome." A slender woman who looked like a 1920s pinup greeted them. "Take a look at my portfolio, and I'll be with you guys in a minute."

It was a small shop and surprisingly clean, with hand-scraped wooden floors. Savannah had never set foot in a tattoo parlor before, but Isabella Noble was hot on the tattoo scene. She had graduated from Montana State with an art degree; the walls of her shop were lined with art awards, her degree and enlarged pictures of some of her best tattoo work.

While Isabella finished up with the client in her chair, Savannah and her entourage gathered around the glass counter and flipped through the tattoo artist's portfolio.

"Wow." Savannah was genuinely impressed with the level of talent Isabella demonstrated in her work.

"Told you," Jessie said before she spun away to explore.

"She'll be able to do Sammy justice," Shayna agreed.

Justine kept silent—her sister would give her moral support, but she wouldn't act like she agreed with the idea if she didn't.

"Look at this one." Savannah pointed to a black-

and-white portrait that Isabella had tattooed on a man's arm. "It looks just like a photograph."

They waited for Isabella to finish, and then it was Savannah's turn to talk to the artist about the tattoo of her dreams.

"Who's this handsome fellow?" Isabella admired the photograph of Samuel.

"My son. Sammy."

They discussed the size of the portrait, the position on her body, and whether she wanted the tattoo to be color or black and white.

"I can do it," Isabella told her. "I'll just need some time to draw it up for you."

Savannah left a deposit with Isabella and set an appointment to come back and get the tattoo.

"Thank you, Isabella." Savannah shook the petite artist's hand. "I can't wait."

Savannah hugged her sister and her friend, and then she walked to her truck with Jessie.

"You know what I was thinking?" Jessie asked her.

"No telling."

"I was thinking that you and my brother should have a vow renewal. Wouldn't that be super cool?"

The thought hadn't crossed her mind, yet it wasn't a bad idea. In fact, it was a pretty fabulous idea. Bruce and she could start over—truly start their marriage anew.

"You could get a new dress—I could be one of your maids of honor again, but this time I could wear a bangin' dress. We could have a huge party at the ranch. You should totally do it."

* * *

"How does it look?" Savannah was lying facedown on the bed, naked to the waist. "Do you like it?"

Bruce sat down next to his wife on the bed, amazed at the likeness of his son on Savannah's back. He took the top off some ointment, squeezed a little onto his clean fingers and rubbed it over the tattoo.

"It looks just like Sammy," he told her. "I love it."

"I do, too. It hurt like all get-out, but it was worth it."

Bruce was glad that Savannah had opted not to put his date of death beneath the portrait—he couldn't be sure, but he felt that his wife had him in mind when she opted to just include Sammy's name and "Beloved Son" with the picture.

Savannah rolled over and then sat up. Bruce's eyes, slightly narrowed, admired her naked breasts.

"You are beautiful, my love." Bruce traced the curve of her breast.

"I'm glad you think so."

"I do." He leaned down and took her breast in his mouth.

The moment his mouth touched her breast, that delicate, sensitive core of her body, right at the apex of her thighs, responded to her husband's invitation. Bruce pulled her on to his lap, suckling her breast until she was moving her hips against him, seeking that relief that only he could give her. With one arm, Bruce lifted her up and sat her down on the edge of the bed. He reached for his zipper, but she pushed his hand away.

With a sensual smile in her eyes, she hooked her finger into his waistband and pulled him between her thighs. She unbuttoned and unzipped his jeans like she was unwrapping a present; his erection, so hard, so warm, sprung free as she pushed his jeans and underwear downward so he could step out of them.

She took him in her hands, stroking him in just the way he loved, before taking him into her mouth. Bruce dug his fingers into her hair and moaned. It didn't take Bruce long to change the position—he enjoyed that type of kiss, but he loved being inside of her.

He held out his hand to her, helped her up, and then took her place on the bed. "Come here."

Savannah knelt on her knees on either side of his muscular thighs and then sank downward, taking him in, letting him fill her so completely. With a little struggle, she untucked her legs so she would wind them around her husband. She wrapped her legs and arms tightly around her handsome rancher, kissing his neck, breathing in his scent, while they rocked their bodies in that familiar rhythm as their moans of pleasure melded together.

After the lovemaking, they lay beside each other in the bed, surrounded by their canine family; Savannah was on her stomach so she wouldn't hurt her new tattoo, while Bruce was on his back, one arm behind his head, the other on her derriere. It was dark in the bedroom, cool and quiet. Their eyes had adjusted to the lower light, so Savannah could still make out the expression on her husband's face.

"Jessie had a crazy idea."

"What's that?"

"She thinks…" Why was she so nervous about saying this? "She thinks that we should have a vow renewal."

Her heart started to beat a little faster when he didn't answer right away. Didn't he *want* to marry her again?

"You mean—like a ceremony?"

Savannah pushed upright and sat cross-legged next to her lounging husband. The more she had thought about a vow renewal, the more excited she was about the prospect. It was a chance to recommit themselves to the marriage, a sign that, no matter what, they were a bonded pair for the rest of their lives.

"Yes." She nodded enthusiastically. "The whole she-bang. A second wedding. I could get a dress. You could be in a tuxedo. We could have a reception here at the ranch for all of our family and friends.

"What do you think?" She reached out to hold his hand.

"I think…" he replied slowly, deliberately. "I'm going to have to go ring shopping."

His brother Liam, a strong supporter of his attempts to repair his marriage with Savannah, met him at the Jewelry Station in downtown Bozeman. The fact that he had a second chance at picking out a ring, proposing and having a ceremony with his wife made Bruce feel hopeful for the longevity of his marriage in a way he hadn't before. To pull back from the precipice of divorce, to have a new opportunity to make Savannah his wife for the rest of his life was, quite frankly, a blessing.

"What are you thinking about getting her this time?" Liam, the tallest of his full brothers and a large-animal veterinarian, was wearing the blue scrubs he usually wore when he conducted pre-purchase vet checks on horses.

"I'll know it when I see it," Bruce told him, scouring the rows of glass cases for the exact ring for his bride.

She was such an extraordinary woman, he wanted this ring to reflect that. And he certainly wanted this new ring to be completely different from the single band of diamonds she wore as a wedding band. She had wanted a yellow sapphire for her engagement ring the first time around, which he had agreed to, but this time, she was going to get a diamond.

"Hello, gentlemen." A pretty blonde woman in her mid-forties greeted them. "What are we looking for today?"

"An engagement ring," Bruce told her. "For my wife."

Tiffany was the woman's name, and she spent an hour with him, showing him different engagement rings and wedding sets. Her patience and expertise were exactly what he needed to finally decide on the perfect ring for his bride. He couldn't find it in the cases; instead, with Tiffany's help and creative skills, he designed a custom diamond ring for Savannah. It was going to be unlike anything she had in her jewelry box—it was going to be delicate and sparkly and fit for a princess. It was going to be perfect for her; he couldn't wait to see it finished. In the meantime, he needed to plan the perfect surprise proposal. He had to think of what would make it special for Savannah—how would she want him to propose?

"Thanks for doing this with me," Bruce said to his brother as they left the jewelry store.

"I'm happy to see you making it work with Savannah," his younger brother said. "I wouldn't wish divorce on my worst enemy."

His own divorce was still a sensitive topic for Liam.

"How are the kids?"

"They seem to be happy enough," the veterinarian told him. "But I get real tired of having a relationship with my own children on a screen."

They gave each other a hug before they parted ways. Liam had been through his own private hell, so Bruce didn't say what had popped into his mind when his brother talked about his children. Maybe it wasn't ideal, but it was better that Liam could still see his children, while he didn't have that luxury; if he could have Sammy back but only see him via video chat, he'd take that deal every day and twice on Sunday.

"Is it true that you aren't coming back this year?" her friend Deb asked her while they began the chore of packing the belongings in her apartment. This task was long overdue, and in light of the progress she had made in her marriage to Bruce, and in light of the fact that it was time to renew her lease, Savannah decided it was way past time to give up her apartment and move all of her belongings back to Sugar Creek.

"It's true," she replied while taping up the bottom of a book box.

Soon after she had found out about Sammy—his life and his death—her desire to shape a different future for herself emerged. Yes, she loved teaching. But her soul wanted something else now. She wanted to start a foundation in Sammy's memory, to build awareness about keeping children safe near all types of water, including toilet and tub. She wanted Sammy to have new life, to be remembered always, and to help other parents not experience the same preventable tragedy. In short, she wanted to dedicate her life to Sammy's memory—it made her feel more connected to the son she couldn't remember, the son she only knew through pictures and family stories and videos.

"Well," Deb said with a sad expression, "we'll miss you. But I do understand. And if there's anything I can do to help with the foundation, just let me know."

She worked all day on the apartment, packing up the kitchen and the bathroom and the living room. It was a hard task, not just physically, but mentally. Inevitably, she came across memorabilia of her relationship with Leroy—cards, notes, printed out pictures hung on the refrigerator. One by one, Savannah destroyed those items and threw them in the trash. Leroy wasn't a bad-looking guy; he was just young and a little uneducated and naive. Why in the world had she gravitated to him? It didn't make a bit of sense; she had a feeling that it never would.

"That's it." Savannah taped up the last box.

Deb was sitting on the floor drinking a soda; her friend gestured for her to join her.

"Here's to you and Bruce." Deb first handed her a bottle of soda and then held out her bottle for a toast.

"I'll drink to that." She clinked her plastic bottle to Deb's.

They were both too tired to expend energy on small talk; they had been friends for years, so they could sit in comfortable silence.

Savannah looked around at the apartment she didn't remember living in. "I can't thank you enough, Deb. I'd still be putting boxes together if you hadn't helped. Now all that's left to do is to get Bruce and his brothers to pack this stuff up, then I can clean it and turn in my keys."

The two of them rested and recharged their batteries

before they parted ways. Deb had to make dinner for her three boys, and Savannah wanted to get back to the ranch to see Bruce. She couldn't wait to tell him that she was ready for him to come get all of her stuff from the apartment. On the "undo the mess we made of our marriage" checklist, getting rid of her postseparation apartment, a symbol to the both of them, was about to be checked right off that list.

After dinner, they went for their usual evening walk. This was one of her favorite moments in her day—walking, hand in hand, along the roads of Sugar Creek Ranch, or through the pastures, with their dogs running and barking and chasing each other. It was such an enjoyable way to end their day together, and it also gave them an opportunity to discuss things that they had on their minds.

They reached one of the fences facing west, and Bruce lifted her up and set her down on the top plank. Savannah spun around so she was facing westward, and Bruce, still standing, leaned against the fence beside her.

She reached over to brush his hair, a little on the long side now, off his forehead.

"The apartment is ready to go."

"I'm glad to hear that." Her husband wrapped his arm around her hips. "I'll get the bros together, and we'll get all of your stuff back on the ranch where it belongs."

"I'm ready."

He nodded.

"I also told Deb about not returning to teaching. It feels weird to say that out loud."

She had always had a career—work had always been her joy—but the foundation for Sammy was speaking to her heart now.

"Do you think I'm doing the right thing?" she asked Bruce. "I mean, about starting the foundation?"

"I want you to follow your heart, my love," her husband said earnestly. "I want you to be happy and I want you to be with me. Other than those two things, I'm flexible."

She leaned down and kissed his lips. "Thank you. Sometimes I think I'm being really selfish leaving my kids at work."

"You're not being selfish," Bruce disagreed. "You're being a mother who loves her son. You're being a mother who wants to stay connected to your son, to have Sammy's life touch other parents. That's not selfish. Personally, I'm really proud of you."

This was classic Bruce—he always made her feel good about following her dreams. Would he be on board about the next dream she wanted to pursue?

"I also made an appointment with my ob-gyn today."

Bruce's brows drew together with concern. "Why? What's wrong?"

"Nothing." She shook her head. "I want to talk to her about getting off the pill."

She had Bruce's full attention now.

Savannah turned a bit so she could look into her husband's stunning blue eyes.

"I want to try to have another baby, Bruce."

His expression was inscrutable—she couldn't tell if he thought the idea was crazy or awesome.

"What do you...think about that idea?" she prompted him.

Samuel had been unplanned, but she could see from the pictures that she had reveled in motherhood. She wished she could remember what it was like to "feel" motherhood and remember what it felt like to hold her son and experience that wide, ecstatic smile on her face. Savannah realized that they would never be able to fill the void that Sammy left in their lives, but why couldn't they bring another life into the family? Why couldn't they create another life, a child manifested from their love, their friendship, their passion and their devotion? Why?

"I think," Bruce finally said, his voice gruff with emotion, "that I would be honored to have another child with you."

Chapter Twelve

"You look handsome." Savannah admired her husband.

He was showered, shaved and dressed in dark blue jeans with a black button-down shirt, and the cowboy hat he only wore on special occasions.

"Thank you, darlin'." He tipped his hat to her. "You're lookin' mighty fine yourself."

Wearing new slender-fit jeans and high-heel cowgirl boots, she gave her husband a little spin so he could get the full effect.

"You're a good-looking woman, my love." Bruce hooked his arm around her waist, dipped her and kissed her lips.

Savannah laughed and wiped her lipstick off her husband's mouth. "That lipstick is not in your color wheel."

She grabbed her handbag, and they left for an evening out on the town. One of Bruce's brothers, Shane, a retired marine and more-often-than-not recluse, was making a rare appearance at a bar downtown. Savannah loved all of her brothers-in-law—even Colton, who still treated her like enemy number one—but she had just a little extra special in her heart for Shane. He had always been such a warmhearted, gentle, sensitive young man who poured himself into his music. All of those things that Shane couldn't say out loud, he said with his voice, his lyrics and his acoustic guitar. After being deployed to Iraq four times, Shane wasn't the same young man. The death and the horrors of war had changed him forever.

At a small, round table, Savannah sat beside her husband, waiting for Shane to begin performing. Every available Brand was present—from Jock to Colton to Liam. Only Jessie, who was still underage, and Noah, who was still in South Korea, weren't in attendance. That was something that Savannah could always say about the family she had married into—they were dysfunctional as all get-out, but they stuck together despite the dysfunction.

"Here he is." Savannah squeezed Bruce's arm excitedly. "Here he is."

"He looks real rough."

Bruce was right about that—Shane looked worse for wear. His hair was long and shaggy, and he had an unkempt beard and mustache. His sunglasses, in her opinion, were a way of hiding his hurt spirit and the bloodshot eyes. Too much booze, too much pot, not enough sunshine and fresh air.

"My name's Shane Brand." Sitting alone on the

stage with a microphone and his guitar, Shane seemed more at home in a dive bar than anywhere else. "I'm gonna play for you folks for a minute or two. I hope y'all enjoy it."

Savannah downed the rest of her beer and nodded her head when Bruce asked her if she wanted another.

"Why do I feel so nervous for him?" she whispered to her husband.

"You've got a kind heart, that's why."

She stopped talking then, her attention on Shane's gravelly, haunting voice and lyrics, so raw and honest that it made her catch her breath a time or two. Song after song, Shane played for the attentive crowd. There was something about Shane that grabbed a person's attention and held on to it for dear life. Between songs, Shane reached down to take a swig of the beer that sat at his feet, or take a drag off a cigarette.

"He's so talented," Savannah said sadly. "But, God, he's so screwed up."

After the set, Shane slumped into a chair at Jock and Lilly's table, a cigarette clenched between his teeth and a fresh bottle of beer in his hand.

Savannah waited her turn, but she finally got to hug her favorite brother-in-law.

"Bruce and I are renewing our vows, Shane." She knelt down beside his chair. "Now I know you don't really *do* family events, but I want you to promise me you're going to come."

Shane, still wearing his sunglasses to cover his eyes, blew out a thin line of white smoke before he said, "I'll do my best."

She stood up and touched his arm lightly. "That's all anybody can ask of you, Shane."

The beer was running right through her, so she excused herself to the bathroom. The line for the women's bathroom, as usual, was long and moving at a snail's pace. She finally got into a stall, took care of her bladder and then stopped at the two-sink counter to wash her hands and check her makeup.

"Well, look who it is. Savannah Brand."

Savannah was midway through glossing her lips when a voice from the past interrupted her string of thoughts about trying to figure out how Bruce and she could support Shane, to help him get healthy again.

In the mirror, Savannah looked behind her and there stood the tall, curvy, always a knockout no matter the decade Kerri Mahoney.

"Hello, Kerri," she said as she slipped the wand back into the tube and dropped the lip gloss into her purse.

They had gone to elementary school, middle school, high school and college together. Kerri had always been the most popular, the most pretty, the most everything, while she had been the sort of cute, sort of quirky, brainy geek girl. Kerri didn't have anything to be jealous of Savannah about, except for the fact that Bruce fell in love with her, put a ring on it and then married her.

Kerri stepped out of line to join her at the sink; the blonde smiled at her own reflection and flipped her thick, shiny hair over her shoulders.

"That's some scar," Bruce's ex-girlfriend observed.

Savannah would always have a daily reminder of the accident with that scar; perhaps it would fade over time, but it would never truly go away. Bruce didn't care two straws about the scar, but Savannah hated it. She had tried to cover it with makeup; Kerri had a talent for finding a person's weakness and using it against them. Yes, Kerri was beautiful on the outside—that beauty did not, however, penetrate Kerri's heart.

Savannah turned away from the mirror. "Bruce doesn't mind it."

Hate, genuine hate, flashed in Kerri's cornflower-blue eyes, before she shuttered the emotion. There was no sense wasting time on a woman who didn't wish her or her marriage well. So, she turned to the side to press past the women in line.

Kerri reached out, wrapped her fingers around the upper part of Savannah's arm and squeezed. "Just so you know—Bruce was in my bed the night of your accident."

Savannah yanked her arm out of Kerri's grip. "That's old news, Kerri."

Shaking with adrenaline and anger, Savannah returned to the table, sat down, chugged her beer then slammed the bottle down on the table.

"What's wrong?"

Savannah nodded to the blonde walking out of the bathroom.

Bruce saw Kerri, and that was all the information he needed. "I'm sorry."

"I'm not," she said, her eyes flashing. "This is a real small town. It was bound to happen."

It wasn't her suggestion, but Bruce wanted to leave once he realized that his ex was lurking near his family's tables. They said goodbye to the family, promised to be at Sunday breakfast, and then, holding her husband's hand, she followed him out of the bar and into the warm Montana night.

"It's still early." Bruce opened the passenger door for her. "What's your pleasure, my love?"

"I want to go home. Maybe toast some marshmallows in the fire pit?"

Bruce shut the door behind her. "We can do this."

Seeing Kerri at the bar had brought up some bad thoughts in Bruce's mind. He liked to ignore the past and just look forward with Savannah—would that ever be truly possible with Leroy and Kerri living in the same small town?

"I've got beer and a half a bag of marshmallows." Savannah came out of the house followed by Hound Dog.

Her hair was in a ponytail, she was wearing a ribbed tank top braless, and her cutoff jean shorts showed off her nicely shaped legs. No, she may not be model gorgeous like Kerri, but Bruce only had eyes for his pretty wife with the gap between her front teeth and a brain that rivaled any he'd ever met, man or woman. Savannah, for whatever reason, spoke to him on a soul-to-soul level that went much deeper than just mere outside appearances.

"I like the way you fill out that shirt," Bruce said with a teasing wink as he accepted a bottle of beer from his wife.

Savannah smiled at him flirtatiously. She had taken off her bra as much to please him as for comfort; she knew he was partial to her shapely, perky breasts.

His wife took a seat next to him on the outdoor love seat by the fire pit. She clinked her bottle to his.

"Here's to us," Savannah said, then took a healthy swig from her beer.

"To us."

Bruce had downed one beer and was on to the next, while Savannah toasted two marshmallows, one stacked on top of the other, over the fire.

"Oh, crap!" She pulled the marshmallows away from the pit and blew out the flame.

"Here." He reached over and slid the burned, gooey marshmallows off the stick. "I like 'em charred."

She wrinkled her nose at him. "I worry about your taste buds. I really do."

With sticky marshmallow on his lips, he buried his face in her neck and started to kiss her ear to make her squeal.

"I like how you taste," he said suggestively, looking downward.

Savannah laughed, and how he loved to make her laugh. Her laugh sounded light and airy, like wind chimes blowing in the wind.

"This is so much better than the bar. The smoke was really starting to get to me." Savannah loaded two more marshmallows onto her stick.

"Why don't you just put one there and that way you'll be able to have more control?" he suggested.

She frowned at him playfully. "Are you giving me advice on how to toast a marshmallow?"

"I think I'm onto something."

"I think you need to just sit back, drink your beer and let me handle the toasting."

They sat outside together, drinking their way through a six-pack of beer and eating too many marsh-mallows to avoid feeling sick later. It was the perfect night at home with his wife; it was the type of night that almost wiped thoughts of Kerri and Leroy and the divorce out of his mind. Almost.

"Wait here." Bruce stood up and swayed a bit from the beers. "I'll be back in a minute."

"I'm not moving from this spot," Savannah said in a singsong voice; she was tipsy, too.

He and a couple of his brothers had moved all of his wife's things out of her apartment; she had cleaned it and turned in the keys, just as she had promised she would. The fact that she was back on the ranch with all of her possessions had made him feel secure and relieved. It made him want to do something equally symbolic.

He returned to his wife and the waning fire in the pit. Savannah was leaning back in the love seat, her legs bent to her chest, her head resting on the cushion.

"I want us to do something." Bruce didn't rejoin her on the love seat.

"What's that?"

He held up the manila envelope for her to see. "I want us to get rid of these."

Savannah pushed herself upright. "What do you have?"

He handed her the envelope. She opened it and slipped the papers out; she glanced quickly over the words, and her eyes widened a bit when she realized she was holding their unsigned divorce decree.

"I don't want them." She handed them back to him.

Bruce held out his hand to her, and she took it.

"Let's burn them together." He held on to her hand.

She nodded; he could tell by the expression in her eyes that seeing the papers had hurt her. They hurt him, too.

Savannah held on to one end of the papers, while he held on to the other end. After a moment of silence, they tossed their divorce decree into the embers. The fire, which had almost died away, began to eat at the paper, burning back the edges of the document and through the center. Bruce wrapped his arms around his wife as they watched the document that had almost ended their marriage turn to ash by the fire.

He couldn't be sure it was the beer, or the thought of how close they had come to destroying their marriage, but he felt, as much as heard, Savannah start to cry.

"Hey..." Still holding her, he bent his head down to look at her face.

Savannah clutched the front of his shirt, the tears from her eyes leaving wet blotches on a favorite button-down.

"We almost lost everything," his wife whispered.

He kissed the top of her head, holding her even more tightly against his body.

"But we didn't," he reassured her. "We're here. Together. Stronger than ever. Aren't we?"

She nodded.

Bruce turned her in his arms, held her away from him, his hands on her shoulders.

"I don't know why I deserve this second chance with you, my love. How did I get so lucky?"

"We both got that second chance."

Bruce looked away, taking a moment to collect his emotions. He looked back to his wife, his eyes taking in the features of the face he loved so much. "I can't seem to forgive myself."

He swallowed hard. "Sammy..."

Instead of pulling away, Savannah stepped closer

to him, wrapped her arms around him and held him as tightly as he had held her.

"You have to forgive yourself, Bruce. You loved our son. You *loved* him."

Bruce rubbed fresh tears out of his eyes. "I miss him. I miss him so much it feels like I can't breathe from it."

Savannah leaned back, put her hand over his heart. "Forgive yourself, Bruce. So we can move on. Forgive yourself—as I have forgiven you."

"Thank you, my love." He took her face in his hands and kissed her lips. "Thank you."

The symbolic burning of their divorce papers was a turning point, a large step forward, in the healing of their relationship. It wasn't perfect, but what marriage was? They had begun to move out of that blissful honeymoon phase, where making love was top on the priority list, and spats were infrequent. Now, it seemed that they were solidly back into the marriage, filled with mundane tasks such as laundry and paying bills and getting the dogs to the vet. They argued more now, but not fights worthy of note. And, they never went to bed mad; they never left a disagreement lingering until the next morning. For Savannah, it was like having her marriage back—just a little bit better, a little bit stronger.

"Good morning, Lilly," Savannah greeted her mother-in-law when she reached the top of the stairs leading up to Lilly's craft loft.

Lilly stood up, hugged her and kissed her on both of her cheeks. "It is a beautiful morning."

Savannah sat down in a chair next to Lilly's crafting table.

"How are the vow renewal plans coming along?" Lilly asked, her fingers nimbly beading a bracelet as she carried on the conversation.

"Great so far."

They had both agreed that they wanted to renew their vows at Story Mansion. They had their first ceremony at Sugar Creek; it had been blue skies and gentle breezes, mountains in the background. They had a lovely souvenir wedding album that they both enjoyed. This time, they wanted something totally different, and they both agreed that getting married at the place where they had first fallen in love *was* that place.

"We're going to have the ceremony at Story Mansion—I've already booked the date."

"What date did you choose?"

"Sammy's birthday."

Lilly looked up from her beading. "That will be a blessing."

"We were worried that some of our family and friends wouldn't understand why we wanted to do that, but in the end, it's really about us. And we want Sammy to be a big part of that day."

"As he should be."

"Do you think that Jock will agree to having a reception here at the main house?"

"Yes, I think so." Lilly nodded. "You are one of his two favored daughters."

Savannah smiled at that. Jock was such a hard man, a difficult man and a flawed man who did not always have the respect of his children. But for some unknown reason she wasn't about to spend too much time questioning, Jock adored her. And he was always kind to her.

"And what shall you wear?"

"That's what I wanted to talk to you about."

She had married Bruce in a simple A-line white lace wedding dress with cap sleeves. She had loved her dress, but in keeping with the "change" theme of their vow renewal, Savannah wanted to wear a dress that was unique, and unusual, and totally unexpected. That was her marriage to Bruce in a nutshell.

"Would you consider making my vow renewal dress?"

Lilly's hands stilled. "You want me to make your dress?"

"I'd like a dress that no one else has ever had. I was thinking of a cross between an American traditional wedding dress and a traditional Chippewa-Cree jingle dress." Savannah lifted her hand. "But only if it wouldn't be considered disrespectful to your tribe."

A jingle dress was a powwow ceremonial sheath, typically made from vibrant-colored fabric, and decorated with rows of shells, metal cones and ornate beading. Savannah had often admired Lilly's ceremonial jingle dresses; it was in her heart to marry Bruce in an outfit influenced by the beauty and symbolism of a jingle dress. Jingle dresses, also called prayer dresses, were considered to be healing garments, and for Savannah, the vow renewal was all about the healing of her marriage.

"I would be so happy to make this dress for you."

Savannah scrolled through some images on her phone and showed one to Lilly. "I think this jingle dress could be made to look like a wedding dress."

Lilly began to sketch some ideas for her daughter-in-law; it amazed Savannah how easily the idea for a dress materialized on Lilly's sketch pad.

"How about this?" Lilly showed her the finished drawing. "When you walk, the dress will sing."

"I love it." She hugged Lilly. "It's so special. Thank you."

Lilly took her measurements and promised to get started on the dress right away. Before Savannah left the craft loft, Lilly selected a bangle she had recently designed and beaded.

"I saw you wearing this bracelet in a dream." Bruce's mother slipped the bangle onto her wrist. "Wear it day and night, and it will bring you much luck."

Chapter Thirteen

"Here she is." Tiffany walked out from the back of the jewelry store carrying a small black box.

The jeweler turned the box around, lifted the lid, and presented the custom diamond engagement ring to him. Inside of the box was a one-carat heart-shaped diamond, surrounded by a diamond halo and set in a delicately embellished white band. It was a Tiffany setting, with the diamond set high up off the band.

"It turned out even more antiquey and princessy than I thought it would."

A small light on the ceiling of the box shone down on the ring, making the center diamond sparkle. For the second time he proposed to Savannah, this was the perfect ring.

"Perfect," Bruce told the jewelry designer. "It's amazing. She's going to love it."

"I know she will," Tiffany agreed. "Do you know when you're going to give it to her?"

"Tonight. We're having dinner with her family, and I'm going to find the right time to give it to her."

"Well—" the jeweler put the ring box into a small, fancy bag with rope handles and gold embossing on the front "—I'm glad that we could be a part of this. Bring her by so we can see how the ring looks on her finger."

"I'll do that."

He wanted the moment to be perfect—Savannah deserved that. Bruce had to admit he wasn't always as romantic as his wife merited, but he did try. All day, while he was out fixing fences and worming the cattle, his mind was on the incredible vow renewal ring he had bought for his wife. It was fancier than she typically liked to wear, a bit flashier than her usual taste. Until he saw her face, until he saw her eyes and her smile, he would be worried that Savannah wouldn't love it as much as he did.

"So, tonight's the night." Colton had ridden up on one of his favorite quarter horses.

"Tonight is the night." Bruce poured some water over his face to cool it off and wash the sweat out of his eyes.

Colton just couldn't move on from the pain Savannah had caused him by leaving the ranch. He understood that; he loved his brother, but this wasn't Colt's decision. This was his decision. And when push came to shove, whether Colton had to fake it to make it or not, he expected his brother to respect his decision and respect his wife.

His younger brother shook his head. "I just don't

get what you're doing here, brother. She left you. She walked. Shacked up with another dude. And now you guys are renewing your vows. You needed her when Sammy died." Colt pointed away from his body. "What did she do? What did she *do*? She kicked dirt in your face, man. I don't care if the whole family wants to act like everything is fine and dandy. That's bull crap, and you damn well know it!"

Bruce let his brother say his piece. That was what brothers did. But when he was finished, he made his point clear.

"She's my wife. I love her. I forgive her." Bruce stabbed his pointer finger into the palm of his other hand. "And God willing, she's forgiven *me*.

"Now...you can hate her guts. That's your right. You *will* treat her with the respect she deserves as my wife, Colt. I don't want to have a problem with you, but we will have a problem if you step out of line with Savannah."

"Mom! Dad! We're here!" Savannah was always happy to be spending time with her family.

Savannah scooped up the family cat and carried him into the kitchen where her mom was cooking up a storm.

"Hi, baby girl." Carol's plump cheeks were flushed from the heat of the stove. "Hi, Bruce."

"Hey, Mom." Bruce hugged his mother-in-law. From the very beginning to right now, Carol had been a big supporter of their marriage. He could always count on Carol to be in his corner.

"Smells delicious, Mom." Savannah smooched

the kitty on the face before putting him down on the ground gently. "Where's Dad?"

"I sent him to the store with a list."

"We could have stopped for you." Savannah snatched a caramelized onion from the pan.

Carol wiped her hand on a dish towel, then hung it over the sink faucet. "I needed to give him a job. I don't know what we're going to do when he retires, Lord help us both. He hovers!"

"Mom." Savannah frowned at her mom.

"I'm not saying that I don't love your father," Carol clarified. "I'm saying that a little space strengthens a marriage. Trust me. The two of you will see when you've been married as many decades as I have."

"God willing." Bruce snuck a couple of caramelized onions out of the same pan.

"All right…okay." Savannah's mother waved her hands in a shooing motion. "Now the two of you are hovering. Go find your sister."

Savannah's sister, Justine, was outside on the deck with her fiancé, high school coach Mike Miller. Savannah was very close to her sisters; they screamed like they hadn't seen each other in years when they got together, and they hugged like they were never going to see each other again. Her strong family values, along with her intelligence that kept him on his toes, were some of the things that made Savannah such a rare find and such a perfect fit for him. He liked that his wife was smarter than he was; he liked the fact that Savannah challenged him to be a better man.

While Savannah and her sister caught up, Bruce excused himself back into the house.

"She's happy again, Bruce," his mother-in-law said plainly. "I haven't seen her smile like that in a very long time."

"When she's happy, I'm happy."

"That's the way family works," Carol acknowledged. "If your spouse is happy, if your kids are happy, you're happy."

"I wanted to show you the ring," Bruce said in a lowered voice.

Carol's face lit up with excitement. She clapped her hands together. Bruce had worn his shirt untucked so Savannah wouldn't spot the shape of the box bulging in his front pocket; he tugged the box out of his pocket and then lifted the lid for Carol to see.

"Oh! Oh!" Savannah's mother's eyes teared up. "Oh, Bruce. It's the most beautiful ring I've ever seen. It truly is."

"Do you think Savannah will love it?"

Carol had her hands on her cheeks. "She's going to feel like the most loved woman in all of Montana."

Bruce hid the ring on the top shelf of one of Carol's kitchen cabinets; the cabinet wasn't often used, so there wasn't a risk of Savannah accidentally finding it.

"You'll give it to her after dessert?" his mother-in-law asked.

"I think so," he told her. "Joy has an early evening class, and I want to make sure we can get her on video chat so she can be a part of it, too."

Carol stopped talking and just started hugging him.

"We are so blessed to have you, Bruce." She used the dish towel to dry her eyes. "Thank you for never giving up on our Savannah."

* * *

It was a festive dinner—everyone was in a good mood, even Savannah's father, who had been slow to accept Bruce back into the fold. A gift of fresh steaks for the grill, straight from Sugar Creek stock, went a long way to ease the relationship with his father-in-law. John cooked the steaks on the grill, taking orders from the family and drinking beer.

They sat down at the picnic table on the deck that they used all summer long in good weather. The center of the table was teeming with bowls filled with potato salad, macaroni salad, hot rolls, green beans, collard greens and mashed potatoes. Carol really knew how to throw together a feast for a family gathering, and Bruce had sincerely missed her cooking during the separation.

"Make sure you save room for dessert," Carol warned the family. "I didn't sweat in that kitchen all day to have my dessert go to waste."

"It's store-bought," John teased his wife.

"Hush your mouth." Carol lifted her chin in feigned outrage. "I would *never…*"

Everyone chipped in clearing the table, stacking dishes in the warm soapy water in the large farm sink; Justine put the coffee on while Carol took the store-bought desserts out of their boxes and put them on serving plates. After the table was cleared and reset for dessert, and the coffee had been brewed, the family converged once again at the picnic table. By now, the sun had set, and a sliver of moon was seemingly floating overhead, a small, yellow slice in a vast, blue-black Montana sky.

"You tell Jock that he can send over steaks anytime."

John had a bit of a slur to his voice. "I missed those steaks while the two of you were separated."

"Dad…" Savannah objected. "That's not even half-way nice."

"It's honest," Bruce said.

"Not polite," Justine added to the discussion. "But honest. Dad, I think that's gonna have to be in the running for your tombstone."

John frowned playfully at his daughters, then to his wife, he said, "You raised a couple of smart-asses, Carol."

Even though they were all stuffed from the meal, every single one of them found something from the pastry assortment to eat for dessert. Savannah finished her chocolate minipastry, wiped her mouth, then tapped her glass with her knife.

"I have a couple of announcements."

Once she had the family's attention, his wife said, "I quit my job."

The joviality seemed to be sucked right out of the air; John's frown was back, and Carol appeared to be both confused, as if she had heard her daughter wrong, and speechless. His father-in-law immediately turned his attention to him—before they were married, he had wanted Savannah to be a stay-at-home wife and mother, while he provided for the family. Yes, it was an old-fashioned model of marriage—a model that he immediately kicked to the curb when Savannah made it clear she wasn't going to play June Cleaver to his Ward Cleaver.

"This wasn't Bruce's decision." His wife was quick to dispel that notion.

"Did you suggest it?" John demanded, that familiar scowl back on his fleshy face. Savannah's father wanted all of his girls to use their brains and stay in school until they received a terminal degree in their field. He didn't care if they gave him grandchildren; he cared that they made something of themselves and stood on their own without the help of a man.

"No," Bruce replied, firmly but still respectfully. He had no intention of starting another cold war with Savannah's father.

"This is—" Savannah gestured to her chest "—*my* choice."

"You love your job!" her sister interjected. "What about your kids?"

"I'm not the only good teacher. They'll get along just fine without me. My heart wants something else now. I want to do something in Sammy's memory."

"Savannah has been exploring the idea of starting a foundation in Sammy's name."

"Well—I *love* that idea," Carol conceded.

"Which brings me to my second announcement."

"How many more of these do you have?" John asked in a caustic tone.

Carol, as she always did, tried to smooth things over between her girls and their father. It was, as far as Bruce could tell, a constant chore.

Undaunted, Savannah smiled, showing her dimples. "A couple more."

His wife reached for his hand, and with a glimmer in her pretty hazel eyes, Savannah announced that they were going to try to get pregnant.

That announcement had the desired impact—Carol and Justine left their seats to give Savannah a hug. A baby was always good for changing a sour mood sweet.

"I'm no longer taking birth control, so…" Savannah caught his eye. "I could be pregnant before our vow renewal."

The rest of the conversation surrounded the plans for the vow renewal, including the date, which elicited a divided response from the family, as well as the venue. After the conversation lagged, the family cleared the table for the final time that night, and everyone seemed to need a break. John went out to his garage with Justine's boyfriend while Justine and Savannah went for a stroll around the neighborhood to walk off some of the calories they had consumed. Bruce helped Carol in the kitchen, rinsing off the dishes and loading them into the dishwasher.

"It's going to take at least two loads," Bruce told his mother-in-law, who was wiping down the kitchen countertops.

"At least," she agreed.

Bruce opened the kitchen cabinet and retrieved the diamond ring. "I think the family has had too much excitement for one night."

"Oh…" she said, disappointed. "I wanted to see her face when she opened the box."

He understood, and he sympathized, but John was pissed off about Savannah quitting her job, and the last thing he wanted was his father-in-law's sourpuss face ruining his proposal. No. He would give Savannah her ring in private; maybe it would be all the more special for it.

"Look at my belly." Savannah was lying flat on her back, surround by canine friends, her shirt lifted up to just below her breasts, her jeans unbuttoned and unzipped. Her stomach was distended, as if she were a couple of months pregnant.

"Total food baby."

Bruce lay down on the bed on his stomach and kissed her belly. "You look beautiful to me."

"I suppose that's all that really matters." She brushed his hair off his forehead with her fingers. "You seriously need a haircut, cowboy."

Bruce captured her hand and brought it to his lips. "Come outside with me for a minute."

"I could stand another walk." Savannah sat up with an uncomfortable groan, then swung her legs off the side of the bed.

Holding Bruce's hand, she followed behind him as they walked out onto the deck. He put his arm around her, and they ambled down the stairs and into their backyard.

"I can't remember a night lovelier than tonight." She marveled at the majesty of the dark Montana sky.

Bruce turned her in his arms, took her face in his hands and kissed her—so softly, so lovingly, that it made her want to cry with joy.

His eyes roamed her face, the way Bruce Brand had always looked at her, as if she were the most beautiful woman in the world, even though all evidence said that she wasn't. She believed that look in his eyes; she trusted the love she saw in those bright, Brand blue eyes.

"I have never seen a woman lovelier than you," he said and then kissed her again. "I can't believe that I've been given this second chance with you, my love. I have no idea what I did to deserve you…"

Before she could respond, before she could tell him

that she was just as lucky to have this second chance with him as he was with her, Bruce did the unexpected and bent down on one knee. There beneath the starless, expansive cobalt-blue sky, her husband, a man she loved to the moon and back, held up a box he had pulled out of his front pocket.

"Savannah Georgia Brand…" Bruce flipped the top of the box open; a strategically placed tiny white light in the box shone down on the stunning heart-shaped diamond solitaire, letting the jewel show off its facets with sparkles of red and purple and blue.

"Will you marry me? Again?"

For a moment, she couldn't speak for the emotion. She didn't wipe away her tears of happiness when she nodded her head quickly, and said, "Yes. Of course. Yes!"

Bruce stood up, took the ring out of the box, and slipped the twinkling diamond engagement ring on the finger of her left hand.

"Oh, Bruce…" Savannah stared at the diamond on her finger. "It's the most beautiful ring I've ever seen in my whole entire life."

"You like it?"

"Are you kidding?" Her voice rose an octave and cracked. "I *love* it!"

"It's a little more…flashy than what you wear… I was worried I'd gotten it wrong."

"No. You didn't." Savannah couldn't take her eyes off her new ring. "It's everything I didn't even know I wanted."

With a squeal of sheer joy, she threw her arms around Bruce's neck and kissed him hard on the mouth.

Her husband lifted her up with one arm, kissed her again and swung her around in a circle.

"We're engaged!" Savannah laughed, her stomach demanding that she stop spinning.

"Married." Bruce let her slide down his body until her feet were firmly back on the ground. "And engaged."

That night, their lovemaking began in the shower and finished in the bed. Now that she had stopped taking her birth control and had begun taking prenatal vitamins, they both wanted to make love as much, and as often, as possible.

"I can't remember when I was pregnant with Sammy," Savannah said quietly, her body curled into Bruce's body, wearing nothing but her new diamond ring. "So when I get pregnant again, it will feel like the first time."

Bruce ran his hand up and down her shoulder. "Does that upset you? That it will feel like the first time, I mean?"

She nodded before her words followed. "Yes. I'm sure it will. What was I like when I was pregnant with Sammy?"

Bruce laughed lightly, his eyes closed. "You were really grouchy. I mean *really* grouchy. But so frickin' cute. You didn't have to buy maternity clothes until the very end of your pregnancy, and that really ticked you off."

"I was mad because I wasn't *big* enough?" She lifted her head to look at him. "That's just flat-out weird.

"What else?" She prodded him.

"You craved marinated mushrooms and buttercream frosting."

"Oh—*God*. Yuck. That's disgusting! Together?"

"No. Thankfully."

She could tell Bruce was about to fall asleep—his voice was increasingly groggy and muffled, he wasn't holding up his end of the conversation, and his eyes had been closed for several minutes. But she had other things in mind. She ran her hand down his stomach and took his flaccid penis in her hands.

"Hmm." Her husband made an interested noise.

"Is it too late to make a withdrawal?" she asked him playfully.

He turned his head toward her on the pillow and kissed the top of her head, still not opening his eyes.

"No, ma'am. It's not."

Chapter Fourteen

"Oh, Lilly…" Savannah stared at her reflection in the full-length mirror. "It's incredible."

Lilly had been working tirelessly on her jingle-inspired vow renewal gown. The dress was made of white cloth and was heavily embellished with rows of silver metal cones and ornate flat-stitch bead work on the sleeves, all of which created lovely flower-shaped bursts of turquoise, red, magenta and yellow, with a wide belt cinching the waist. On the bottom hem, a row of fringe gave the long sheath dress a bit of interest around her calves.

Savannah shifted her hips side to side, and the dress made its own sort of music, like wind chimes in a gentle breeze.

"I feel strong in this dress," she told her mother-in-law. "Like I can face anything and survive."

Lilly had offered to make her a pair of matching moccasins, but Savannah wanted her outfit to represent all of her—she chose to wear a pair of cream cowgirl boots, hand-crafted, with a tapered high heel.

"I am so glad that you like it." Lilly smiled at her with her dark brown eyes.

"It's…" She felt herself start to choke up with emotion. Today she would marry the man of her dreams, her best friend, lover and father of her children—for a second time. "It's more than I could have ever expected. You are so talented."

Lilly hugged her, kissed her lovingly on the cheek, and then left the cabin to return to the main house to get ready for the ceremony. Her mother and her two sisters passed Lilly on her way out, and Savannah started to laugh by herself in the bedroom at the sound of her family's loud, excited voices filling the tall rafters of her log cabin.

Savannah walked down the hallway, swinging her hips so her jingle dress would jingle, and met the women in her life in the living room.

"What do you think?" She spun around to show off her outfit.

"Now, *that* is a dress!" Joy, in town for the weekend, ran over to her and gave her a big hug. "You look ah-maze-ing!"

"Oh, sweetheart." Carol started to cry. "I've never seen you look more beautiful."

"Here." Justine handed their mom a tissue.

"Better just hand her the box." Joy laughed.

Her mother and sisters shuffled her off to the bedroom so they could carefully remove the dress until after her hair and makeup were done.

"I'm *here*!" Jessie screamed, while at the same time slamming the front door. "Let's get this party started!"

Savannah was pampered and prepped by the women in her life. Joy slicked her hair back off her face and created a single, simple twist. With such an ornate, special dress, she wanted her hair and her makeup to be subtle.

Jessie, up on the latest in makeup trends, took care of making her face look youthful and dewy. By the time she was all dolled up, she hardly recognized herself in the mirror.

"I look like the woman Bruce will want to marry twice."

"You look like a woman my brother is gonna knock up tonight," Jessie said from her perch on their bathroom counter.

"Lord have mercy." Carol's peaches-and-cream complexion turned pink.

"Well…" Justine gave her a look of approval. "Let's go get you *renewed*, sis."

"What's goin' on with this stupid thing?" Bruce couldn't seem to get his silver-and-turquoise bolero tie, a gift from Lilly, to cooperate.

"Let me do it." Liam bent his knees a bit so he could take a closer look. "There."

Bruce turned to look at his reflection; he'd gotten married in jeans the first time around—this time, he was wearing a tuxedo. Savannah always wanted to see him in a tuxedo, and what better time than this ceremony to renew their commitment to each other. This was the day, a day long awaited, that he would dedicate his life, his heart and all of his days to Savannah.

"Well, this is as good as it's gonna get." Bruce shrugged. His recent haircut was a little too short for his liking, and the tuxedo made him feel like he couldn't much move his arms. Hopefully, Savannah would be impressed when she first saw him. That would make all of the discomfort worth it.

"Here." Colton came in with a couple of aspirin and a glass of water. "This'll help you feel better."

"Thanks, brother." Bruce took the aspirin gratefully. His frat brothers and his blood brothers had taken him out the night before, and his head felt like someone was hitting him in the temple with a ball hammer.

Savannah had warned him not to go out and get drunk with his brothers, and he hadn't really intended to do that. A couple hours into the evening, hopping from one old haunt to the next, all of the drinks his brothers were buying him had started to blend into one big drink. No, he hadn't gone out looking to get drunk, but he surely had achieved that goal.

"My wife is going to have my head on a stick if I show up looking like something the dog threw up."

"You're kinda jaundiced." Like a unicorn, Shane was making a rare family appearance. Bruce was glad to see him, but he smelled strongly of marijuana. Lilly and Jock would not be pleased.

"Thanks, bro." Bruce had noticed that his skin was an odd shade of yellow. "'Preciate it."

A loud burp followed those words; why—*why*—had he indulged last night? If Savannah sensed how sick he felt, he was going to begin their marriage reboot with a seriously ticked-off wife.

"You ready to head out?" Liam came out of the bathroom, dressed now in his tuxedo. Liam had been his best man during their wedding ceremony; it meant a lot to have him standing beside him for the vow renewal.

"Let's do this." Bruce had to fake it to make it, and he would. Savannah was counting on him.

Bruce walked up the path to the porch of Story Mansion, and was greeted by his friends and his family awaiting the start of the ceremony. He entered the mansion with so much history and so many of his own memories. The building had been restored to its early 1900 glory—with wide-plank wood floors and thick, unpainted crown molding—and the air smelled of wood polish and fresh paint.

"Mom." Bruce hugged Lilly, who had chosen to dress in a traditional ceremonial Chippewa-Cree gown and moccasins, with her silver-streaked hair deliberately styled into two long braids.

"Son." Lilly pressed her cheek to his. This was their way.

With Liam standing beside him, somewhere down the hall, an antique grandfather clock chimed four times. It was time for Bruce to see his bride—it was time.

Bruce heard his wife approaching before he saw her; the jingle dress foretold her arrival. At the entrance to the turret room, Savannah stood between her father and her mother.

"Damn…" Bruce said under his breath. "That's my wife."

The moment he laid eyes on his wife, wearing an ornate jingle dress made by his mother's talented hands, thoughts of his acid stomach and his pounding head disappeared into the recesses of his mind. All he could think of was the ethereal, angelic, powerful, badass woman who was his bride.

Savannah kissed her father and her mother, and then walked the short distance to him on her own. Her dress jingled charmingly with every step she took toward him. Her smiling eyes were on his, holding him with the look of unadulterated love.

He took several steps to her, reached out for her hand and walked with her, together, the rest of the way to the spot where they would, once again, pledge their lives to each other. They'd opted to write their own vows, just their words, without a pastor.

Liam took his seat after he hugged Savannah, and then it was just the two of them, facing each other, hand in hand.

"You look handsome." Savannah smiled up at him with a gentle, sweet, accepting smile.

"You are beautiful."

This was the moment—it was time, in front of God and all of his friends and family, to tell Savannah how much she was loved by him.

"Savannah. My beautiful, brilliant wife. I love you, a little bit more every day. I stand before you now, a lucky man, a blessed man, because of your love in my life. I have promised to love you, in sickness and health, for richer and poorer, until death us do part. I reaffirm that vow to you now. I promise you that I intend to spend the rest of my days on earth being worthy of your love."

Jessie sneaked forward and pushed a handkerchief into Savannah's hand. Savannah laughed, which broke a little bit of the tension in the room, and carefully dabbed the tears from her eyes, trying valiantly not to smear her makeup.

"Thank you." She gave her sister-in-law a quick sideways glance.

"Bruce," Savannah began, a catch in her throat that she had to clear before she continued. "I am so proud to be your wife. You are my best friend, the love of my life. You have my heart, Bruce—my whole heart. My life doesn't work without you. I vow to always love you, to always be by your side, no matter what comes our way." Savannah held his gaze and repeated, "No matter what comes our way."

Bruce took her face in his hands and sealed their vows with a kiss. Savannah laughed through fresh tears and wiped her lip gloss from his lips.

"I love you, Bruce," she said. "So very much."

Their friends and family were clapping loudly, cat-calling and whistling. Bruce barely heard them.

"I love you more."

They took pictures inside the mansion and on the grounds surrounding the historical home. Then the entire party of friends and family headed back to Sugar Creek for a Montana-style shindig. They had a band, a dance floor put down, and plenty of food and drinks. They requested that, instead of gifts, their attendees contributed money to the GoFundMe page that Savannah had started for Sammy Smiles—the foundation that she was determined to create in their son's memory.

"Here." Jock opened up his son's jacket and slipped an envelope into the inside pocket. His father rested his hand on top of the jacket, then gave him one single pat on the chest. "That's for Samuel."

"Thank you," he told his father. "It means the world to Savannah."

He'd managed to lose his wife shortly after they arrived back at the ranch, but he found her near the stage speaking to his younger brother, Shane.

Bruce shook his brother's hand. "I'm glad you came."

"Shane's going to play for us later," Savannah told him.

"Everyone'd really like that." He put his arm around his wife's shoulder. "I'm going to steal her for now."

Bruce led his bride out onto the dance floor, and spun her around until she walked into his embrace.

"Are you happy?" he asked her as they danced slow even though the music was fast.

"So happy." She rested her head on his chest.

They danced and drank and ate until midnight arrived, and Shane sat down on the piano bench; her favorite brother spoke in a low voice, in between puffs on a cigarette, to the band. After a minute, he adjusted the microphone and asked for everyone's attention.

Bruce and Savannah stood next to the stage, their arms circling each other.

"Most of you know that I don't do covers." Shane spoke in a raspy voice as the crowd gathered around the stage. "But this here's Savannah's favorite song, so I'm gonna play it for you folks right now."

Shane's hands on the keyboard, her troubled, talented brother-in-law said, "I love you, Savannah. Bruce."

As they stood, wrapped in each other's arms, their

friends and family all around, Shane began to play the piano and sing, in that haunting, rough, damaged-deep-in-his-soul voice, Eric Clapton's "Wonderful Tonight."

The crowd was mesmerized by Shane's rendition of a classic song; everyone was so quiet until he took his hands off the keys and put the half-smoked cigarette burning on the edge of the piano back into his mouth.

"Thank you," Shane said before he stood up. "Take care of each other."

Before they could catch him and say thank-you for the song, Shane disappeared into the crowd, and undoubtedly returned to his garage apartment, his safe zone, back in town.

Savannah tried to stifle a yawn, but Bruce felt as tired as she looked at this point. This day had been incredible, but the planning of such a big event had been exhausting for them both.

"We need to go to bed, my love. We have an early flight and a long journey."

She nodded her head in agreement. They began to make the rounds, saying good-night and thanking everyone who had been such an important part of their day. They had one last champagne toast with their guests, then they turned in with their dog pack. With his help, Savannah carefully took off her dress and hung it in a protective garment bag.

He came up behind her, brushed her hair off her neck and kissed the warm, sweet-smelling skin he'd uncovered.

"You looked wonderful tonight," he told her, repeating the words of her favorite song.

She turned in his arms and held on to him, her head on his chest, her arms wrapped tightly around his body.

"I love you more than words can say, Bruce."

He took her face in his hands, his eyes sweeping the lovely features. "That makes me the luckiest man in Montana, my love. The luckiest man."

"I can't believe we went to bed without fooling around on our vow renewal day." Savannah brought him a cup of coffee while he packed the last toiletries into his carry-on bag.

"Don't you worry your pretty little head about that." Bruce took a sip of the coffee. "We're going to more than make up for it on our trip."

"When are you going to tell me where we're going?"

"I already gave you a hint."

"A ridiculous hint."

He laughed. "You won't need a bathing suit, but you can bring one if you want. That's a great clue."

"No." She frowned at him playfully. "It's not."

They both took turns hugging and kissing their dogs before they dropped them off at the main house. They headed to the airport and that was when Savannah finally got to find out where Bruce had been planning, for a long time now, to take her for their vow renewal honeymoon.

"Oh. My. God!" Savannah grabbed his arm and pushed it back and forth excitedly. "Fiji? You're taking me to *Fiji*?"

"That's where you always wanted to go, isn't it?"

"Are you trying to make me fall in love with you all over again, Mr. Brand?"

Bruce gave her a quick kiss on the lips. "You'd better believe it."

* * *

It was a long day of traveling, and she had never been much of an airplane person. The seats were too cramped; there were too many people coughing. She was more concerned about the germs recycling throughout the cabin than she was of crashing, oddly enough. But by the time they were close enough to Fiji to see those legendary sapphire-and-turquoise blue waters, Savannah forgot about her germ concern and just focused on all of the amazing adventures she was going to have with her husband in the most amazing paradise on the planet.

Bruce had booked a private bungalow on Turtle Island. They would have access to their own private beach, opportunities to hike, bike, snorkel, surf, sunbathe in the nude and lounge in their own hot tub.

"We have to get couples massages at the spa." Savannah pointed to a picture in the dog-eared brochure she had been reading and rereading to pass the time on the plane.

"I don't like people touching my feet." Bruce gave a little shake of his head. "Can I keep my boots on?"

Savannah smacked him with the brochure. "When in Fiji."

They took a pontoon plane for the final leg of the journey to the five-hundred-acre privately owned Fijian island called Turtle Island, which was one of twenty volcanic islands in the western division of Fiji. They were going to be in paradise for two glorious weeks, and because the island was privately owned, they would have the run of it, and the utmost privacy on the beach dedicated for their bungalow. Bruce wasn't a fan of the idea, but she fully intended to get naked on the beach. She had always wanted to frolic on the beach in her birthday suit; this might be her one and only opportunity to have access to a totally private beach.

"This. Is. Amazing! Look at this place!"

They were shown to their accommodations by their own private butler, or Bure Mama, who would take care of their every need during their stay. Their villa, named the Ratu Mara Bure for a former Fiji president, was a thatched, vaulted-roof bungalow, hand-constructed from hardwood indigenous to the island by local artisans; the Ratu Mara was designed for luxury and complete privacy. Only one of fourteen tucked away in the tropical foliage with a view of their own completely private slice of white-sand beach, it was better than she had imagined. The pictures in the brochure, as beautifully done as they were, did not, *could* not do the real magic of Turtle Island justice. The native hardwood gave off a sweet scent that mingled with the salty breeze blowing in from the beach. The first thing she did after she hugged and kissed her husband for finding them the perfect spot to celebrate their marriage reboot, was yank off her boots and socks and run out to the beach.

"Come with me!" she called to Bruce.

Her husband sat down on a chaise lounge chair on their private deck, removed his boots and socks and followed her out to the beach.

Savannah tilted her head back, suddenly not feeling the least bit fatigued from the nearly twelve-hour plane ride, reached out her arms and spun around in the sand.

"I am so happy!"

Bruce scooped her up and continued to spin her.

They both ended up dizzy and laughing, sitting on the beach.

"We are in paradise together," she said in amazement.

"Yes, we are."

Savannah linked her arm with her husband's and dug her toes into the white, sugary sand. "You know I'm going to sunbathe on this beach in the altogether, don't you?"

Bruce squinted his eyes against the sun. "I know."

"I think you should get naked with me—let it all hang out."

"I think that's a solid 'no.'" Her husband's answer was swift. "All of my altogether will be neatly tucked away in proper attire."

Savannah jumped up, started to walk down to the water's edge and called out to him, "You know what, Brand? You can be a real prude."

Bruce followed her, scooped her up in his arms and began to run toward the water.

"Are you ready to get wet?"

Savannah squealed, kicked her legs and laughed and wrapped her arms around his neck. She wanted to make sure that if she ended up in the water, Bruce ended up in the water with her.

Her husband carried her into the water, turned around so his back was to the water and sank down with her still in his arms. Wet, fully clothed, they wrapped their arms around each other and kissed the water from their lips.

Savannah felt her husband's arousal, so hard, so fast. She wrapped her legs around his hips, and pressed her groin to his.

"Okay—we need to either, one, go back to our villa—" she licked the salty water from his neck and nibbled his ear "—or, make love to me right here, right now."

Chapter Fifteen

They did consummate their vow renewal that night, in the balmy air drifting into their bure while they bound their bodies together and loved each other as an expression of their deep and abiding connection. And then they slept. Nothing had ever felt so peaceful, being lulled to sleep in their king-sized bed, with a rhythmic breeze brushing over their bodies bringing a scent of tropical flowers, growing wild all around the bure, mingled with the fresh, salty smell of the water of the Pacific Rim.

Savannah rolled over onto her back, bringing one of her three pillows with her. She blinked her eyes several times, trying to adjust them to the bright light being brought into the villa by the late-morning sun.

"What time is it?" Her voice sounded a little raspy, and she prayed that she was just tired from the past months of her life instead of experiencing the first sign of an "airplane cold."

Bruce was sitting at the built-in desk, looking at his laptop. "Eleven-fifteen."

"Oh, my God," She yawned loudly, stretched and then turned on her side and snuggled back into the mattress and pillows. "I can't believe I slept that long. When did you get up?"

Her husband had yet to turn toward her, his attention still mainly on the computer screen.

"Around nine. I went for a walk around the island."

"Did you eat?"

He nodded.

"Well…" She yawned again. "I'm starving."

Another nod.

This *would not* do! They were *literally* in paradise—her husband was going to unplug from technology while they were there. Savannah threw back the covers, forced herself to get her body moving as she swung her legs out of bed. Naked, she walked over to where Bruce was sitting, gave him a hug and a kiss on the cheek, before she reached over his shoulder, slammed the laptop shut and then took it.

"Hold up!" Bruce finally turned to look at her. "I was answering an email."

"No," she said forcefully, holding the laptop behind her back. "We are in *Fiji*! You need to stop working on things that can keep for two weeks and focus all of your attention on what really matters."

As if noticing for the first time that she was standing naked before him, Bruce's eyes swept over her body, lingering on her breasts, the curve of her waist, and the small patch of hair at the spot where her thighs met.

"What's that?" Bruce's slightly narrowed, sexually interested gaze was back on her eyes.

"Me." Savannah laughed. She clutched the laptop to her chest, spun around and ran to the other side of the bed.

Bruce always loved a good chase, and he easily caught her near the bed and pulled the laptop out of her hands—but instead of taking the computer back to the desk, he put it on the night table and took her to bed instead.

Her pushed her back onto the mattress playfully; one breast he massaged in a way he knew she enjoyed, while he began to kiss the other breast, taking the nipple into his mouth.

Laughing, Savannah escaped from his grasp. "You've got to feed me first, Brand. I need energy to keep up with you!"

Their Bure Mama made sure she had a breakfast fit for a queen brought to the villa. Savannah feasted on passion fruit, guavas, star fruit and papayas. She drank two large cups of coffee, and then she felt ready to get up and enjoy the natural gifts of Turtle Island.

Dressed in a modest bikini, Savannah handed her husband a bottle of sunscreen. He was dressed in a T-shirt, bathing suit trunks and his standard boots had been replaced with a pair of flip-flops.

"You do me, and then I'll do you."

Living in Montana, even during the summer months, there were places on their bodies that just didn't see the light of day. They both had superpale legs and stomachs, while their necks and arms were a shade or two darker.

"We have to really work hard not to get burned," she

told him while he rubbed coconut-scented sunscreen on her back, her derriere and her shoulders.

They went down to their private beach, which made it seem like they were the only two humans in the Garden of Eden. The Bure Mama had a two-person lounge chair brought to their private beach at their request.

"Oh, Bruce." Savannah sighed, her eyes closed, the sun on her face. "Thank you."

In response, her husband took her hand and squeezed her fingers, his version of "you're welcome." Their first full day on the South Sea island paradise was perfection; they relaxed, vacillating between the lounge chair and the cooling sea-foam-green and turquoise-blue water. Every second of that first day was theirs; no schedule, no reminders of the past, no stress. Just the two of them, together, in what had to be one of the most beautiful places on the planet.

After a day at the beach, they took showers and got dressed for a surprise planned by Bruce. Feeling more free and sensual on this remote South Sea island than she had at any other time in her life, Savannah slipped into a lightweight minidress with spaghetti straps. Her legs had been turned gold with a pink undertone, but it didn't hurt. She opted to go commando beneath her dress and as she turned around in front of the mirror, making the filmy skirt of her dress float away from her body, she felt so sexy. She hoped Bruce agreed.

Hand in hand, they walked down to the water's edge of the island's Blue Lagoon, a cove protected from the waves, and that was when she saw a pontoon floating in the calm water, with a table for two, lit only by lanterns lining the boat.

"Is that for us?" Savannah squeezed her husband's hand in excitement.

"Yes." Bruce sounded proud of himself for keeping the secret—and for pleasing her.

A boat carried them to the pontoon; their food would also be brought to them by the same boat. Together, by the light of the lanterns, they feasted on seafood and vegetables picked that day from the island's garden. They filled their bellies with Pacific green lobster, cooked to perfection, and caught a nice buzz from the sweet red wine.

Their empty plates had been removed, and now they sat at their table with a 360-degree water view, drinking a last glass of wine.

"I will never forget this, Bruce," she whispered, feeling like the space was too sacred to speak in a full voice.

"You deserve this, my love." They touched glasses one last time. "Here's to second chances."

"Yes," she agreed softly. "To second chances."

They walked back to their villa from the Blue Lagoon, and once again, they were completely alone. Savannah had kicked off her sandals and was dangling them from two fingers, swinging them as they walked the beach. Hand in hand, they strolled along the water's edge, with the only light given off by the nearly full moon hanging in the clear night sky.

They reached the part of the beach directly in front of their villa.

"Let's get a towel and sit on the beach," she suggested.

She was glad that her rancher, who was typically

set in his ways as far as extracurricular activities, was being more open to her ideas than usual. Bruce put on his swim trunks, just in case they wanted to get into the water, and picked up a couple of towels for them.

Savannah chose a spot close enough to the water to enjoy the sound of the gentle waves rolling to shore, but far enough away that they wouldn't get wet if they chose to stay dry. Perhaps it was the dreamlike, mystic charm of the island, or perhaps it was the fact that she was in a place where her wildest desires were possible, but Savannah felt like she couldn't put off the experience of being her natural self in this place that was raw and wild in a way that she had never known before. Savannah stood up and pulled her dress over her head and dropped it onto the towel at her feet.

She closed her eyes, stretched her arms high above her head, her naked flesh completely exposed to the elements. Empowered and free. These were the two words that came to mind as she stood, unclothed, with the soft ocean breeze brushing over her breasts, her thighs, her face.

Bruce was quiet beside her; he didn't approve, but he wasn't going to try to stop her. This was one of her bucket list items; he knew her well enough to know that she knew her own mind, and she followed her own heart.

"Bruce!" She stepped off the towel and sank her toes into the cool, damp sand. "You should try this!"

"I'll live vicariously through you, my love." He had leaned back on his elbow and was admiring the view of her naked body in the moonlight.

"You'd love it." She spun around, her arms open wide. "I love you."

* * *

One of the most memorable moments of his life, he was certain of it, was watching his wife, naked as the day she was born, wearing only her heart-shaped diamond and a smile, frolicking on their Fijian beach. This trip had set him back a pretty penny, but it was worth everything he had spent and more. Money could not buy the happiness on Savannah's face; she was like a kid in a proverbial candy store. She wanted to taste everything, make friends with all of the Fijian people, drink as much as she could manage and experience every activity the island had to offer. She already had them scheduled for couples Lomi Lomi massages and Ulumu facials at the resort spa; she had also signed them up for snorkeling, a sunset cruise, windsurfing lessons and stand-up paddleboard lessons. He'd rather not tackle any of those activities, but he wanted to please Savannah. He wanted to make her smile and then keep her smiling. So he'd had to hang up his cowboy hat and put up his cowboy boots, and learn how to step out of his Montana rancher box.

"You're beautiful!" he called out to Savannah, who was currently executing rather impressive naked cartwheels and handstands.

He was always turned on by his wife's naked body; this moment was no different. Bruce had to shift his position to make the erection in his swim trunks a little less annoying. There was no way the hard-on was going away; he couldn't keep his eyes off Savannah. Her sun-kissed flesh in the moonlight, her hair blowing wildly around her pretty face, her breasts bouncing enticingly with every step she took.

Bruce stood up and walked over to Savannah, who

was standing at the water's edge, letting the ocean lap over her bare feet.

From behind, he wrapped his arms around her body and kissed her sweet-smelling neck.

Savannah reached up and put her hands on his arms, leaning her body back. "Hi."

"Hi."

Bruce, unable to wait a minute longer to have her, lifted her into his arms and carried her back to the towel. He laid her down on her back, lightly running his hand over her breasts, her stomach, until his fingers were nested between her thighs.

"Hmm." Savannah arched her back and tilted her hips upward toward his hand. "Yes, please."

Bruce then did something he swore he wouldn't do—he untied his swimming trunks and stripped them off. The more he watched his wife playing on the beach, her naked body glowing in the yellow light, the more he wanted to make love to her right here, on this secluded spot.

"You're so handsome." Savannah admired him through heavy-lidded eyes.

He lay down beside her, leaned on one elbow so he could hover just above her, and kissed her with all of the pent-up passion he felt. She reached between them to wrap her fingers around his hard penis; he reached between them so he could slip his fingers in her hot, slick center.

She stretched for him, pulling him forward, signaling that she was ready for more—that she needed more. Quietly, their breaths mingling as they gently kissed each other's lips, Bruce guided himself into her body, joining them as one being. Buried all the way inside of his wife, he lifted himself up, his elbows locked so he could watch her face. Every little movement of hips made her gasp.

"Is this what you wanted?" he asked her, their eyes locked in the moonlight.

"Yes." She gasped again, reaching for him, pulling him downward so he would give her the weight of his body.

They moved together, adopting the rolling rhythm of the ocean, each giving the other as much pleasure as they received. She came first, her cry of ecstasy caught by the breeze.

"I feel you," Savannah whispered into his ear, sending a shiver down his spine. "I feel you."

Those sensual whispers sent him over the edge; he thrust deep inside of her and exploded with a primal scream, unlike any sound he'd ever made during lovemaking in his life.

Savannah had her legs wrapped around his back as he let her take his weight, for just a minute, while he caught his breath. Holding on to her, he rolled their bodies so she was on top of him, her head on his chest, his nose breathing in the coconut scent in her hair.

"That was amazing." Savannah laughed, her fingers buried in his chest hair.

"Agreed."

They stayed on the beach, curled in each other's arms, until they were both so tired that they feared falling asleep there. Groggy and satiated, they ambled back to their villa, rinsed the sugary sand off their bodies and then climbed, completely spent, into the canopy king-sized bed.

* * *

"Well?" Savannah was staring at him like a cat watching a fishbowl.

"What do you want me to say?" he asked her.

They had just had their Lomi Lomi massages, considered to be an ancient healing massage, a living Aloha, first practiced in Hawaii.

"Did you *like* it?"

Bruce was glad to be dressed again; he wanted to get the heck out of the Vonu Spa.

Savannah's face was glowing from her facial, and she seemed to be perfectly languid and relaxed by the Lomi Lomi.

Now outside of the spa and far away from any ears that could be offended by what he was about to say, Bruce said in a harsh whisper, "They double teamed me!"

Savannah laughed, her head thrown back, her eyes twinkling at his obvious distress and discomfort.

"Four hands. *Four* hands!" He hadn't really been all that thrilled with two strange hands massaging him; his wife had been very strategic about *not* telling him that there would be *four* strange hands involved in the Lomi Lomi.

"They touched my feet! Both of them."

"Both of your feet? Or both women?"

"Both!" he snapped. "It felt like an assault!"

Savannah kept on laughing; she grabbed his hand and swung their arms.

"You'll be fine," she said with a teasing glint in her eyes. "It was good for you."

"Says who?"

It took several tropical fruit drinks and a lunch of

freshly caught fish to help him recover from his "healing" massage. After lunch, they did something that he had been wanting to do: visit the island's black volcanic cliffs. They took a tour of the cliffs, snapping copious amounts of pictures to post to social media so their friends and family could share in their adventure. After the volcanic cliffs, and now being one week into their two-week vacation, Savannah was starting to crave the company of their fellow Turtle Islanders. They got cleaned up from the day and dressed for the group dinner provided by the resort every night. This would be their first group dinner, and Savannah was beaming with excitement.

"They are going to have native music and dancers perform for us," she told him. "I can't wait. Aren't you excited?"

He raised his eyebrows at his wife, who seemingly could get excited about the smallest of things. "I can't wait."

She rolled her eyes at his lack of enthusiasm, which she had to accept as part of who he was, gripped his arm with her hands and bumped her shoulder into his. "Don't worry. You're gonna love it. I promise."

"Look," he said, only half joking, "after that assault you called a massage earlier, I am going to approach all of the activities you plan for us with caution."

At the group dinner, they were seated next to another couple, two people they had met briefly on a walk along the path through the lush island jungle.

"Hey!" Savannah smiled at the familiar faces, always quick to make a new friend. "We meet again!"

The woman was tall, over six feet at least, slender,

and undeniably beautiful; her features were subtle and balanced, her mouth full and colored a deep red—her skin was the color of light brown, and she wore her raven curls in a loose Afro which added a lovely frame to her pretty face.

With a British accent, the woman greeted them as they joined her and her companion at the table.

"I'm Ivory," she said, introducing herself. "And this is my husband, Miguel."

After the introductions and ordering the food, Savannah started small talk with Ivory and found out that she was a model and a budding fashion designer.

Ivory touched her husband's shoulder. "My husband is my biggest supporter. He picks me up when my chin's dragging on the ground."

"I'd love to see some of your designs," Savannah said to the model. "I love fashion."

Ivory stood up and modeled the boldly patterned sundress. "This is one of mine."

Savannah's eyes lit up. "My sister, Joy—she's the tall one—would look amazing in that dress."

"Tell her to visit my website." Ivory sat down and asked her husband, "Do you have any of my cards, love?"

Miguel, a quiet man much like Bruce, pulled a card from his wallet and handed it to her. Savannah looked at the card before tucking it into her pocket.

"Where are the two of you from?"

"Montana," Savannah told Ivory. "Bruce's family owns a ranch outside of Bozeman."

"I've been to Montana," the British model told them. "One of my best friends is from Montana."

"Small world…" Savannah interjected.

"She's an incredible painter. Maybe you've heard of her?" Ivory continued. "Jordan Brand? Well, Jordan Sterling now."

Savannah was rendered temporarily speechless, and she felt Bruce stiffen next to her. Their branch of the Brand family discussed the other Brand branches so infrequently that she often forgot that they existed.

Not sure exactly how to handle this, Savannah decided to just speak their truth. "Jordan is actually our cousin…mine by marriage"

"You're joking!" Ivory's brown-black eyes opened wider for a split second. "I just saw Jordan last week—she was just at our wedding!"

Chapter Sixteen

The rest of the dinner was filled with small talk, but Savannah was actually glad when the dancers began to perform. After discovering Ivory's connection to their estranged extended family, the rest of this meal felt a bit awkward and strained. In order to salvage the evening and keep Bruce at the table, Savannah quickly shifted the conversation away from the Bent Tree Ranch Brands, out of Helena, Montana, back to Ivory's designing career.

Now back at their villa, Savannah and Bruce both sank down into the hot tub with a bottle of champagne and assorted tropical fruits with melted chocolate for dipping.

"I can't believe that out of every island on the planet, we ended up on a Fijian island with a good friend of your cousin Jordan. How does that even happen?"

Bruce dipped a piece of papaya in the chocolate and held it up for her to eat.

"Hmm," she said between chews. "So good."

Her husband popped a chocolate-covered star fruit into his mouth. "Beats the hell out of me. But when she called us the 'bad Brands,' I had a real hard time holding on to my table manners."

She moved her arms in the bubbling hot water. "I know. How did we become the bad Brands—if Jock's brother hadn't been so greedy after your grandpa died, we'd all probably still be a whole family, don't you think?"

Bruce poured a glass of champagne for her, but she shook her head.

"No, thanks."

"You didn't drink yesterday—you didn't have wine with your dinner. What's going on?"

Savannah drifted over to him, a secretive smile on her face. "Do you remember how worried I was about getting my period while we were here?"

He studied her face carefully. "Yes."

His wife stood up in the hot tub, water rolling down her breasts to her puckered nipples in the most tantalizing way.

"Well—" she ran her hands over her stomach "—I missed my period.

Now he was looking at her stomach—had he planted a baby inside of her?

"I brought two early-detection pregnancy tests," she told him. "If I *am* pregnant, we'll know tomorrow before breakfast."

Bruce wanted so badly for his seed to take hold in his wife's womb. Every time they made love, every time he climaxed, he prayed that this would be the moment when they made another baby together. And he knew that Savannah felt the same way; they had been having sex like hormonal teenagers on this trip. Whenever he wanted it, she wanted it, too; whenever she wanted it, he gave it to her.

He put his empty champagne glass down, leaned his head down to lick the water from her nipples, his hand splayed across her stomach.

"God, I pray you're pregnant, Savannah."

His wife moved onto his lap, their slick bodies coming together so naturally. "I have prayed to God every day to give me your child, Bruce. I want another child with you so badly."

"We aren't going to stop trying until it happens." He dropped gentle kisses on her lips, her cheeks, her eyes. "I promise you that."

When they got too hot from the hot tub, they rinsed off with cold water in their shower, dried themselves, and then got into bed. Quietly, no words were needed, they began to make love again. Savannah rolled onto her stomach and then lifted up on to her knees, offering herself to him. Bruce leaned forward, massaging her back, her hips, and then reaching beneath her body to massage her breasts. He entered her from behind, loving the little gasp she made as he controlled the rhythm and the depth. Holding on to her curvy hips, he thrust forward; he knew the minute he touched her cervix because Savannah began to push back, moaning, writhing her hips, begging for him to come inside her. This was the shortest lovemaking session they had on their trip—it was so quiet, so quick, his climax so intense that it bordered on painful. Spent, he pulled his beloved wife into his arms, pulled the covers over their bodies. Somewhere deep inside, in a place that was as intangible as it was mysterious, Bruce felt that this was the night—this was the moment—that he had given Savannah another child.

They spent the last week in paradise trying to work their way through Savannah's extensive checklist of activities. The morning that his wife had taken a pregnancy test, and it had come back negative, Savannah's spirits slumped. Bruce had made it his mission to lift her spirits and to remind her that they had only been trying for a short time. And wouldn't it be even more special if they could trace the moment of conception back to this amazing island?

They spent the last day on their private beach, lounging, floating in the clear water and doing their best to soak in those last precious moments of their time in Fiji. That night, their last night, they packed up their belongings and then had a romantic last dinner for two on their patio.

"Well, let's make one last toast." Savannah held up her glass of water.

Even though she hadn't gotten the news that she had wanted, and she wasn't in fact pregnant, his wife had decided to stop drinking alcohol to prepare for pregnancy.

"To us, my love." Bruce touched his glass to hers. "Thank you for being my wife."

She smiled, pleased. "I love you."

He took a sip of his wine; he'd discovered on this trip that he actually preferred it to beer.

"I love you more."

After dinner, they took one last walk on the beach. The sky, now that the moon was such a small sliver, was bursting with twinkling white stars.

"Do you think that we'll ever come back here?" his wife asked—he heard a sadness in her voice that their time on the island was coming to end.

"I don't know." This trip had been a once-in-a-lifetime visit that had come with a hefty price tag. He didn't begrudge the expense, but they did have a Montana ranch to run back home, and that wasn't cheap, either.

"Even if we never get to come back—" she tucked her hand into the crook of his arm "—this was such a blessing to be able to come here even once."

That was the moment when they shared a last kiss, on the beach, in the salty air, with the sparkling stars of Fiji twinkling in the cobalt-blue night sky.

Bruce had loved the trip to Fiji, but he was sure glad to be back at Sugar Creek Ranch. Montana was still his idea of paradise. He was back in his jeans and his T-shirts, his cowboy hat and his boots. He'd had his fill of seafood and tropical fruit; he was happy to have grits and eggs on his plate in the morning, and steak and potatoes on his plate at night. Savannah loved the ranch as he did, but he also knew that the transition from Fiji back to Montana had taken her a bit longer.

"Hey," Savannah greeted him when he got done with the day's work. She was sitting cross-legged on their bed, as always surrounded by their canine family members, with her laptop open in front of her.

He gave her a quick peck on the lips, wanting to get in the shower and wash the sweat and grime off his skin.

"I want to show you something when you get out of the shower," she told him.

"Okay."

On the way to the shower, he picked up a pair of Savannah's jeans and a bra.

"Love, why can't you seem to get your clothes near the hamper?" Bruce asked, tossing the dirty clothes into the hamper in their closet.

"Didn't I?" his wife asked distractedly.

Bruce chuckled, half out of disbelief, half out of acceptance. One of the minor prices he would have to pay for being married to Savannah was her chronic inability to get her clothes in the hamper.

He showered, shaved and then joined his family on the bed.

Savannah smiled at him and turned the computer screen so he could see it. It was her GoFundMe page for the Sammy Smiles foundation.

"Is that accurate?" He looked at the large bank of money on the page.

"Yes," she said, her voice emotional. "Our friends and family *and* people who have visited my page out of interest or because they have lost a child themselves to household drownings. One hundred thousand dollars, Bruce. *One hundred thousand.* We have more than enough to get off to a great start."

He leaned over and kissed her lips. "I'm so proud of you."

"Thank you. I'm actually pretty proud of me, too."

* * *

She wanted to say thanks to her friends and family for their generous contributions to Sammy Smiles. So Savannah decided to organize a party as a way of expressing her gratitude but to also talk about next steps. Now that she had more than enough money to set up a nonprofit organization and begin to put the donations to work to save lives, she had to figure out what the heck to do. She had an idea, she had a passion, but she wasn't sure how to best use the money that had been entrusted to her. The truth of it was, she had the money and the idea, and zero experience running a nonprofit.

Even though she didn't have an idea about how to run an organization, she was pretty talented at throwing a fabulous, memorable party. While Bruce spent his days working the ranch, Savannah threw herself into planning an event to unveil the logo design and the website she was having built for Sammy Smiles. The best place she could think to hold the event was Sugar Creek Ranch. Jock and Lilly were always gracious hosts, there was enough space for their guests and the beauty of the swath of land that was Sugar Creek was undeniable.

"Oh, thank you, Dad!" Savannah threw her arms around Jock's neck and kissed him hard on the cheek. "I promise we'll pay for everything, and we'll clean up after ourselves."

"It's for Sammy," Jock said gruffly. Jock had loved that little boy so much; Jock's $25,000 check had gone a long way to get them to that $100,000 mark.

That night, Savannah filled her husband in on the details of the first official Sammy Smiles event.

"It seems like it's all pulling together real nicely," her husband said.

"It really is," she agreed.

After a moment of silence, she posed a question that had been on her mind. "Let me ask you something."

Bruce didn't look up from the game he was playing on his phone. She poked his leg with her toe. "Bruce."

"What?"

"Would you please look up from your game for one second, please?" She knew that she drove him crazy when she didn't pick up her clothes or left the toothpaste cap off the tube, but he drove her just as nuts with his Angry Bird games.

"I'm looking at you."

"I hope it didn't hurt too much," she teased him with a heavy dose of sarcasm.

"Not too much."

"Brat," she retorted. "I really want your advice."

Now he was really looking at her and listening.

"Do you think I should go back to school to learn how to run a nonprofit?"

Bruce thought for a moment. "If you want. Do you think you can handle that and having a child?"

"Tons of women do." She shrugged. "Why can't I?"

"Then I say go for it."

"Really?"

"Really."

Whether he was just placating her so he could get back to his game playing, or if he sincerely thought it was a good idea, didn't really matter. She had asked, he had answered, and she was now positive that she was going to go back to school in order to acquire the skills she needed to run Sammy Smiles and have the foundation have the biggest impact.

"How did you talk Dad into a party this soon?" Jessie, ever pretty and full of energy, asked her.

"I think he was willing because it's for Sammy Smiles."

"I think he was willing because *you* asked," Jessie shot back. "Who's that?"

Savannah looked over to where Jessie was pointing. "That's one of Bruce's SAE brothers."

"Hello, frat boy." Jessie trilled her tongue.

"He's way too old for you, Jessie."

"I only want to play a little, Savannah. Don't be such a killjoy."

There really was no talking Jessie out of anything she was determined to do, and Bruce's fraternity brother didn't stand a chance if Jessie decided to hook him.

Almost everyone who'd RSVP'd showed; the night, a clear, cloudless evening, cooler now that it was fall, was filled with dancing and laughter and eating and catching up. She showed everyone her pictures from Turtle Island, still missing those warm waters and the freedom of making love on the beach, as she scrolled through photos.

"Dance with me." Bruce held out his hand to her.

"Go with him," her friend Deb told her. "We'll catch up some more later."

Her husband led her out onto the dance floor, spun

her into his arms and smiled down at her with appreciative eyes.

"You sure know how to put together one hell of a shindig, Mrs. Brand."

"Everyone seems to be having a good time, don't they?"

"They sure do."

Sometimes, Savannah still had difficulty synthesizing the Savannah before the accident, the one who had lost over three years of memories that never returned, with the Savannah she was now. She still ran into Leroy and Kerri on occasion, but the impact of seeing them was hardly noticeable.

"What are you thinking about?" Bruce interrupted her private thoughts.

"Oh." She shook her head and gave him a little smile. "It's silly. Sometimes I still try to remember something, anything from those lost years."

Her husband's concerned eyes swept her face. "I don't want you to hurt over that anymore, my love."

She tilted her head back so she could look at him with all the love she felt in her eyes. "I don't hurt anymore, Bruce. I have you. I have all of this. I have Sammy Smiles."

The music stopped, they stopped dancing and Bruce kissed her, as he always did, on the lips.

"It's time to make some announcements," Savannah told her husband.

Bruce had his arm around her shoulders; in a low voice meant for her ears only, he asked, "Are you ready for this?"

She leaned back against him, her head touching his shoulder briefly. "I've been ready."

They both climbed the stairs to the stage; Savannah stood behind the microphone, now adjusted for her shorter height, while Bruce stood beside her, ever her support system.

"Good evening!" Savannah greeted everyone at the event. "Is everyone having a great time tonight?"

All of those friendly faces of her family and her dearest friends made her feel the swell of love and kindness she was sending to them reflected right back to her.

"First, I want to say thank-you for all of your generosity. Because of you, Sammy Smiles has been officially registered as a tax-exempt nonprofit organization!"

The crowd cheered and clapped for her; on a large screen behind her, a picture of their sweet son, Samuel, appeared, and the cheering and the clapping grew louder, became more intense.

She had promised herself that she would get through the speech without crying; she had promised herself. But the minute she looked over her shoulder and encountered the larger-than-life face and smile of the son she had lost, the tears wouldn't be denied. The picture she'd selected for this night, and for the logo of Sammy Smiles, was the very first picture she'd seen of her son after the accident. It was the first memory she had of Samuel.

"There's my angel," she said, her eyes lingering on her son's face a moment longer. "Sammy's life, his sweet soul and his incredible smile will live on because of all of you. Sammy's life will never be forgotten, and because Sammy lived, because Sammy smiled, I hope that not one more parent will have to suffer as we have.

And, even though there are still so many memories missing from my mind, the love in my heart for my precious little boy knows no boundaries."

After Savannah unveiled the new Sammy Smiles logo and website, she reached for Bruce's hand and waited for the rowdy, enthusiastic attendees to quiet down.

"Bruce and I have learned that no matter how deep your pain, no matter how large your loss, life does indeed go on."

She glanced up at her husband.

"It is possible to come back from the edge of the abyss. It is possible to forgive and heal and feel joy again."

Bruce squeezed her hand reassuringly as she continued.

"And we are living proof, a testimony to God's grace, that we can stand before you tonight, stronger in our marriage than ever before, and proudly share with all of you that we are, in fact, pregnant."

The shouts of surprise and joy filled Savannah's heart; how could one woman get so lucky twice in one lifetime?

"That's one hell of a souvenir!" someone yelled from the crowd.

"You're damn right it is!" Bruce agreed.

Hand on her stomach, Savannah smiled out at her friends and family. "I believe in my heart that Sammy will be watching over his little brother or little sister from heaven, and I…" She paused as tears of both sadness and joy continued to flow down her cheeks. "I take comfort in that." After the announcements were over, Bruce hopped off the stage and reached back for her. She bent her knees and let her husband swing her down.

Her husband wiped the tears from her cheeks. "Do you have any idea how happy you've made me, my love?"

"Only as happy as you've made me." She leaned into his body, her arms around him, her face tilted up. "I love you."

Bruce, her handsome, strong Montana man, held her face in his hands, his deep blue eyes so full of love for her and their unborn child.

"My beautiful wife," Bruce whispered against her lips, "You know I love you more."

* * * * *

Don't miss the next book in the
BRANDS OF MONTANA *miniseries, coming in*
August 2018 from Harlequin Special Edition!

And catch up with the entire Brand family:

THANKFUL FOR YOU
MEET ME AT THE CHAPEL
HIGH COUNTRY BABY
HIGH COUNTRY CHRISTMAS

Available now wherever Harlequin Special Edition
books and ebooks are sold!

COMING NEXT MONTH FROM

H HARLEQUIN®

SPECIAL EDITION

Available September 19, 2017

#2575 GARRET BRAVO'S RUNAWAY BRIDE
The Bravos of Justice Creek • by Christine Rimmer
When Cami Lockwood, wedding gown and all, stumbles onto his campfire after escaping a wedding she never wanted, Garrett Bravo is determined to send the offbeat heiress on her way as soon as he possibly can. But when she decides to stay, he starts to realize his bachelor status is in danger—and he doesn't even mind.

#2576 A CONARD COUNTY COURTSHIP
Conard County: The Next Generation • by Rachel Lee
Vanessa Welling never wanted to return to Conard City, but an unsought inheritance forces her to face unwelcome memories. But Tim Dawson and his son have dealt with grief of their own and when they open their hearts to Vanessa, she's not sure she'll be able to push them away.

#2577 THE MAVERICK'S RETURN
Montana Mavericks: The Great Family Roundup
by Marie Ferrarella
Daniel Stockton fled Rust Creek after the death of his parents ten years ago. Now he's back and trying to mend fences with his siblings—and Anne Lattimore. But he's about to realize he left more than his high school sweetheart behind all those years ago...

#2578 THE COWBOY WHO GOT AWAY
Celebration, TX • by Nancy Robards Thompson
After years of travel and adventure to find themselves, champion bull rider Jude Campbell and accidental wedding planner Juliette Lowell are reunited in their hometown of Celebration. But will their new hopes and dreams once again get in the way of their chance at a life together?

#2579 DO YOU TAKE THIS BABY?
The Men of Thunder Ridge • by Wendy Warren
When Ethan Ladd becomes guardian to his nephew, he's determined to be the best father he can. There's only one catch: to ensure Cody doesn't end up in foster care, Ethan needs a wife. Luckily, local college professor Gemma Gould is head over heels for baby Cody and is willing to take on a marriage of convenience!

#2580 BIDDING ON THE BACHELOR
Saved by the Blog • by Kerri Carpenter
Recently divorced Carissa Blackwell returns to her hometown and reconnects with her first love, Jasper Dumont—can they rekindle an old flame while the ubiquitous Bayside Blogger reports their every move?

**YOU CAN FIND MORE INFORMATION ON UPCOMING HARLEQUIN® TITLES,
FREE EXCERPTS AND MORE AT WWW.HARLEQUIN.COM.**

HSECNM0917

"Munchy!" Cami cried. The mutt raced to greet her and
she dipped low to meet him.

Garrett waited, giving her all the time she wanted to pet
and praise his dog. When she finally looked at him again,
he explained, "The bear must have whacked him a good
one. When I found him, he was knocked out, but I think
he's fine now."

She submitted to more doggy kisses. "Oh, you sweet
boy. I'm so glad you're all right…"

When she finally stood up again, he handed over the
diamond ring and that giant purse.

"Thank you, Garrett," she said very softly, slipping the
ring into the pocket of the jeans she'd borrowed from him.
"I seem to be saying that a lot lately, but I really do mean
it every time."

"Did you want those high-heeled shoes with the red
soles? I can go back and get them…" When she just shook
her head, he asked, "You sure?" He eyed her bare feet.
"Looks like you might need them."

"I still have your flip-flops. They're up by the Jeep. I kicked them off when I ran after Munch." For a long, sweet moment, they just grinned at each other. Then she said kind of breathlessly, "It all could have gone so terribly wrong."

"But it didn't."

She caught her lower lip between her pretty white teeth. "I was so scared."

"Hey." He brushed a hand along her arm, just to reassure her. "You're okay. And Munch is fine."

She drew in a shaky breath and then, well, somehow it just happened. She dropped the purse. When she reached out, so did he.

He pulled her into his arms and breathed in the scent of her skin, so fresh and sweet with a hint of his own soap and shampoo. He heard the wind through the trees, a bird calling far off—and Munch at their feet, happily panting.

It was a fine moment and he savored the hell out of it.

"Garrett," she whispered, like his name was her secret. And she tucked her blond head under his chin. She felt so good, so soft in all the right places. He wrapped her tighter in his arms and almost wished he would never have to let her go.

Which was crazy. He'd just met her last night, hardly knew her at all. And yesterday she'd almost married some other guy.

Don't miss
GARRETT BRAVO'S RUNAWAY BRIDE
by Christine Rimmer, available October 2017 wherever
Harlequin® Special Edition books and ebooks are sold.

www.Harlequin.com

LOVE
Harlequin romance?

Join our Harlequin community to share your thoughts and connect with other romance readers!

Be the first to find out about promotions, news, and exclusive content!

Sign up for the Harlequin e-newsletter and download a free book from any series at

www.TryHarlequin.com

CONNECT WITH US AT:

Harlequin.com/Community

 Facebook.com/HarlequinBooks

Twitter.com/HarlequinBooks

Instagram.com/HarlequinBooks

Pinterest.com/HarlequinBooks

ReaderService.com

 **HARLEQUIN**®

ROMANCE WHEN YOU NEED IT

HSOCIAL2017

THE WORLD IS BETTER WITH

Romance

Harlequin has everything from contemporary, passionate and heartwarming to suspenseful and inspirational stories.

Whatever your mood,
we have a romance just for you!

Connect with us to find your next great read, special offers and more.

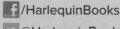 /HarlequinBooks

@HarlequinBooks

www.HarlequinBlog.com

www.Harlequin.com/Newsletters

 **HARLEQUIN**®

A *Romance* FOR EVERY MOOD™

www.Harlequin.com